CW00516893

The Notorious Lola Montez

Jack Falworth

The Notorious Lola Montez
Published by Jack Falworth
Copyright © 2022 Jack Falworth
Cover design by Laura Moyer
(www.thebookcovermachine.com)

All sexual activity depicted in this novel involves characters who are 18 years or older.

CONTENTS

Chapter		Page

CHAPTER ONE

Lola's Early Life

LOLA GILBERT (who later adopted the stage name Lola Montez) was born in Limerick, Ireland. Her father was an officer in the British Army who had distinguished himself for valour during the Napoleonic wars, while her mother claimed to be a descendant of the Count de Montalvo, a Spanish grandee.

Lola was just four years old when her father's regiment was posted to India. The young girl enjoyed her childhood years in India, but shortly after her thirteenth birthday, her parents decided to send her to a boarding school in England, so that she could receive a proper education. The school was Miss Ashley's School for Young Ladies in Sussex, and Lola spent the next five years of her life there without once seeing her parents in faraway India.

At the age of eighteen years, Lola was an astonishingly beautiful young lady. She had a shapely figure with large, firm breasts, narrow waist and long, slender legs. Her hair was jet black in colour, her flashing eyes were a deep blue, while her teeth were sparkling white and perfectly even.

Lola was quite conscious of her striking beauty, and like many other young ladies, her ambition was to marry a wealthy young gentleman, preferably one with a title, who could provide her with a life of luxury and comfort.

One afternoon during her final year at the school, Lola was summoned to Miss Ashley's office.

"Why have you sent for me?" she asked anxiously. "Have I done something wrong?"

"No, you've done nothing wrong," replied Miss Ashley, much to Lola's relief. "I called you, because a letter for you has just arrived."

Lola took the letter which had an Indian post mark, and opened it. The letter was from her mother, the first she had received in more than six months, and it stated:

My dear Lola,

I have written this letter to let you know that I am sailing for England in about ten days. It's been five years since I last saw you, and I intend to take you back with me to India when I return.

I have great plans for your future, and I want to see you reach the top of the social ladder in Calcutta. Place your trust in me and I will arrange everthing.

Your Ever Loving Mother.

Lola was puzzled by the second paragraph of the letter, wondering what her mother's great plans were. She was not sure how her mother intended to help her climb the social ladder in Calcutta, and she reread the letter several times, trying to make sense of it.

In the days before the opening of the Suez Canal, the voyage from India to England around the southern tip of Africa was a long one, and three months passed before Mrs. Gilbert arrived at the school. She was accompanied by a young gentleman in his early thirties, who was wearing a military uniform.

Lola was in class when they arrived, and Miss Ashley sent a maid to the classroom to inform Lola that Mrs. Gilbert was waiting in the school office and eager to see her beloved daughter again after so many years apart.

When Lola entered the office, her mother cried out, "Lola, is it you? My darling child! You have grown so much since I last saw you!"

Rushing forward, Mrs. Gilbert embraced her daughter, kissing her cheeks and forehead. Turning to the young army officer who was standing beside her, she said, "Look at her, Thomas! Isn't she stunning? What woman would not be proud of such a daughter?"

"She certainly is, no mistake about it!" drawled the soldier, his eyes roaming over the curves of Lola's voluptuous body. "But what else would one expect of the daughter of such a beautiful mother?"

"Lola, my dear, let me present Lieutenant Thomas James of the Twenty-first Regiment, Native Infantry, Bengal. We met on the boat."

Lieutenant James bowed, and taking Lola's hand, pressed it to his lips. "I am charmed to meet you, Miss Gilbert," he said. "Bar your mother, I have never met such an angelic creature as yourself."

"Oh, isn't he a nice gentleman!" giggled Lola's mother, who was delighted by the young man's flattery. "Lieutenant James is on sick leave," she went on to explain, "and has returned home to recover from his illness. During the voyage from

India, I did my best to be a good nurse and assist him in his recovery. I must say that I enjoy his company."

"Where is Father?" asked Lola. "You didn't mention him in your letter."

"No, I didn't. Your father has just been promoted to Adjutant General, and he is on very good terms with the new Governor-General. He's been far too busy with his official duties to take any leave, and it'll be years before he does. So I have come to England alone, not that I have really been alone. Lieutenant James has been a good friend, and he never leaves my side."

Mrs. Gilbert proceeded to say that she intended to stay only a month in England before returning to India with Lola. But first she would like to take her daughter to London where they could do some shopping together.

The next day, Mrs. Gilbert, Lola and Lieutenant James travelled by coach to London, where they took rooms in a hotel close to the fashionable shops in Regent Street.

The following morning, Mrs. Gilbert took Lola on a shopping spree, buying gowns, shawls, lingerie, shoes and bonnets for her. The girl was amazed at her mother's generosity, because she had received only a meagre allowance from her mother during her years in the school and had never enjoyed the luxury of fine clothes.

They went from shop to shop, and Lieutenant James trailed along behind, carrying the boxes and parcels of the expensive purchases.

Day after day they went shopping, and Lola became increasingly amazed at her mother's profligacy.

"Mother, why are you buying all these expensive things for me? Why don't you buy some for yourself?"

"A young lady like yourself must be properly outfitted," replied Mrs. Gilbert.

"But the clothes cost so much money," protested Lola.

"Don't worry about the money. You will need the clothes in Calcutta. You can't associate with the best people unless you have fine garments."

Lola was even more astonished when Mrs. Gilbert commenced a tour of the jewellery shops, buying ornate brooches, pearl necklaces, and diamond-studded gold rings.

She was completely amazed by the exorbitant cost of such jewellery and she was now becoming suspicious of her mother's unrestrained spending.

"Mother, where did you get the money to buy all these things?" she asked. "Please tell me what is going on!"

"Don't ask me such questions!" snapped her mother in reply. "I don't have to explain my actions to you or anyone else. You are only a child and you must trust me to do what's best for you."

The very next day, Lola decided to speak to Lieutenant James to find out if he knew what her mother's purpose was. As Mrs. Gilbert and the lieutenant were almost constantly together, Lola did not find an opportunity to approach him until the evening.

As Mrs. Gilbert was feeling tired, she went up to her hotel room after dinner, leaving Lola and the lieutenant alone together in the dining room.

"Thomas," said the young girl "May I ask you a question?"

"Sure," he replied. "What do you want to know?"

"Why has my mother been buying all those expensive clothes and jewellery for me? I don't understand why she thinks I will need them."

"You mean she hasn't told you what her plans for your future are?"

"No, she won't tell me a thing. I'm sure something is wrong, and to tell you the truth, I don't want to go back to India with her."

Thomas hesitated several moments before speaking. At last he said, "I am afraid what I have to say will be a shock to you, Lola."

"Oh, please tell me, Thomas! Please, you must!"

"I wish I could I tell you gently, but I cannot. All those expensive clothes are your trousseau."

"My trousseau!" gasped Lola. "And all that jewellery—and that diamond ring?"

"It is your engagement ring."

"My engagement ring!"

"Yes, your mother has pledged you in marriage to one of the richest men in India."

"She has done what?" cried Lola in disbelief. "Who is this man?"

"You must have known him as a child. He is a judge of the Supreme Court of India—Sir Abraham Lumley."

"Sir Abraham Lumley!" gasped Lola in horror. "Sure, I remember him. He was an old man when I knew him, and he would be even older now. He had a red bloated face, a big nose like a vulture's beak, and small eyes like those of a weasel. He also had a round paunch , and suffered from gout. He is the very last man I would choose as a husband."

"Your mother will be disappointed if you refuse to marry him," remarked the lieutenant. "If you don't do as she wants, she may disown you."

"If she thinks I am going to bow to her will, she is very much mistaken!" spat the young girl. "I am the ruler of my own fate, and I will not allow her to force me into marrying such a revolting creature!"

The very next morning, Lola confronted her mother, who was surprised to see that the young girl was trembling with anger.

"Mother, I know why you bought all those clothes for me," said Lola. "You have arranged my engagement, haven't you? To that filthy creature who used to paw me when I was a child?"

"Oh, so that's it!" cried Mrs. Gilbert. "So Lieutenant James has spilled the beans, has he? I might have known he couldn't keep his mouth shut!"

"You admit it then? You'd sell your own daughter in marriage to that old reprobate!"

"Don't you dare call Sir Abraham an old reprobate!" shouted Mrs. Gilbert. "He is a distinguished member of the peerage and a most respected judge of the Supreme Court of India."

"You know as well as I do he's an old rascal! He gives me the creeps and I would die before I'd ever allow him to touch my body! How could you think of marrying me to him?"

"Sir Abraham is one of the richest and most desirable of all the bachelors in India. You should thank your stars that I've been able to arrange your marriage to him. Any girl who gets him is fixed for life—a title, position, hundreds of thousands of pounds to spend, and——"

"You mean an old man who could drop dead at any moment?"

"Yes, don't I know that?" replied Mrs. Gilbert with a crafty smile. "He has no heirs, and he can't live forever. He's got a weak heart, and when he dies, his widow will inherit everything! Be sensible!"

"No, I refuse to marry such a repulsive man! I won't be sold into this marriage—like a slave!"

"You've got no choice, my darling! You have no means of supporting yourself. The only way for a poor girl like you to get ahead in life is through marriage—the right kind of marriage!"

"Mother," Lola implored, "I won't be thrown into the jaws of what would be worse than death!"

"You little fool! Don't you realize that the marriage settlement has already been arranged. I presented my terms to Sir Abraham and he has agreed. The law gives a parent legal rights over a minor child, and if necessary, I will invoke the law, which will back me up. If you resist, I will have you hauled before a court as a wayward, disobedient child. Before I allow you to spoil what I have done for you, you ungrateful little wretch, I'll see you dead and buried in your grave!"

Lola was shocked by the threatening tone in her mother's voice. She could tell that her mother was implacable. Mrs. Gilbert meant to force Lola to marry Sir Abraham, and the young girl could expect to receive no mercy from her.

"Well, that's enough of these melodramatics," said Mrs. Gilbert. "We will leave London tomorrow and go down to Southampton to board the boat for India. When we arrive in Calcutta, I'm going to make your coming-out party the most brilliant function of the season."

CHAPTER TWO

An Elopement

LOLA GILBERT had no intention of allowing herself to be sacrificed on the altar of her mother's avarice. She therefore sought out Lieutenant James and appealed for his assistance.

After she had explained that she would rather die than marry Sir Abraham Lumley, the lieutenant said, "There is only one way out of your predicament, Lola. You must flee from here tonight."

"But where will I go? I don't know anyone who would give me shelter."

"Yes, you do. I'll take you with me to Ireland, where my sister lives. Your mother won't think of looking for you there."

"But if I run away with you, everyone will think the worst of me. They'll think that I am a shameless hussy who is living with a man outside the bonds of wedlock."

"No, they won't, Lola," said Thomas, clasping her slim body in a warm embrace. "I haven't revealed my feelings to you before, but I must confess that I have fallen madly in love with you. Will you marry me? If you are my wife, I'll become your protector under the law, and you will be safe from your mother."

"Do you really love me?" asked Lola in surprise.

"Yes, I do. Well, what do you say? Do you accept my proposal?"

Lola was flattered by Thomas's proposal of marriage. She was fond of reading romantic novels, and the idea of eloping with a dashing young army officer appealed to her.

"Yes," she said, throwing her arms about his neck. She pulled his head down to hers, their lips fusing together in a long, moist kiss. When their lips parted, she cried, "I love you, Thomas. I could wish for nothing more than to be your wife."

The two of them left the hotel within an hour. Thomas had hired a carriage, and it sped out of London and along the highway towards Bristol, where they bought tickets on the next boat to Dublin.

When they arrived in Ireland, Thomas sought out a parson to marry them, and they were united in the bonds of holy matrimony two days later.

Their wedding night was spent in the old Shamrock Inn in Dublin. After they had enjoyed a meal and a bottle of wine, Thomas led Lola upstairs to their room.

A large bed stood in the middle of the room, which was illuminated by a flickering candelabra. Thomas took Lola in his arms, kissing her on the lips.

At the end of the long kiss, he suggested that she should take off her clothes, and Lola hesitated for some moments. She was still a virgin, and she had never before exposed her naked body to a member of the opposite sex.

"What's wrong?" asked Thomas, a little impatiently. "We are now man and wife, and it is all right for you to undress in the presence of your husband."

"Thomas, please excuse me if I am a little nervous. I will try not to spoil our wedding night."

She removed her garments one by one, revealing her naked charms to Thomas's avid gaze. His eyes roamed from her round breasts, down over her flat belly to her wide hips and long, slender legs. The juncture of her plump thighs was adorned by a triangle of dark curls.

"My God, you do have a lovely body!" cried Thomas, obviously impressed by what he saw.

Without waiting a moment longer, he ripped off his own clothes and Lola gasped when she saw his cock, which was already firmly erect and throbbing eagerly. She stared at it like a mouse hypnotized by a cobra.

Thomas pushed Lola backwards onto the bed, and then threw himself on top of her, inserting the mushroom-shaped head of his prick between the folds of her cleft. He lunged forward, but succeeded in forcing only an inch of his shaft into her sheath before encountering her virginal membrane.

"Ouch, you're hurting me!" cried the girl, surprised at the unexpected pain.

"I'm sorry, Lola," said Thomas. "But your maidenhead must be disposed of first before we can make love. I promise you that the pain will last for only a few seconds, and after that you will experience nothing but pleasure."

"Are you sure, Thomas?"

"Yes, you darling girl. Be brave and try not to struggle."

Lola steeled herself for the pain she must suffer, and Thomas drove his cock forward with one mighty thrust, bursting through her hymen and embedding half the length of his shaft in her sheath. He shoved again and again, driving his cock into her up to the hilt.

Lola bravely endured her ordeal without uttering one cry of complaint. Once his shaft was deep inside her, and the pain from her ruptured maidenhead had subsided, she begged him to grant her the pleasure he had promised.

"Do it to me, Thomas! Come on, do it!"

Thomas was more than willing to oblige. He started moving his cock in and out of her cunt, and the young girl was soon gasping and moaning as she was overwhelmed by voluptuous sensations she had never experienced before.

"Oh, that feels so wonderful!" she cried. "Oh, oh, oh!"

Lola lifted her hips to meet his powerful thrusts, moaning and gasping as Thomas drove his cock deep into her yearning flesh. The two of them were sweating from their exertions, their hot bodies slick with moisture.

Thomas soon speeded up the pace of his strokes, his balls slapping against the soft cheeks of Lola's bottom.

The young bride gurgled with delight as the exquisite sensations in her loins increased in intensity, climbing rapidly towards a crescendo.

"Oh, Thomas!" she gasped. "I feel so strange! Oh, my God! What is happening? I feel as if something is about to explode within me! AH—AH—AARRGGGHHH!!!"

Lola arched her hips up, her body going perfectly rigid for several long seconds, and then jerking and flopping about in the grip of a series of spasmodic convulsions. Her eyes rolled back in their sockets, her head thrashing from side to side.

Thomas spurted off only a few seconds later, flooding the inmost recesses of Lola's belly with burst after burst of sizzling spunk.

They collapsed weakly in each other's arms, and fifteen minutes passed before they recovered from their amorous sport.

"Did you enjoy yourself?" Thomas asked.

"Yes," she replied. "I never before knew that such pleasure was possible. Let's do it again!"

CHAPTER THREE

The Viceregal Ball

LIEUTENANT Thomas James had decided to spend the twelve months of his furlough in Dublin, and he took lodgings close to the army barracks, so that he could carouse with old friends and cronies among the soldiers.

As he was on half-pay while on sick leave, James had little money, and what little he had, he spent in the pubs and gambling dens of Dublin. Much to Lola's dismay, she belatedly realized that she had married a penniless subaltern whose debts far exceeded his meagre income. He went out on sprees with his drinking mates on most evenings, and sometimes did not return from these nocturnal revels until the next morning.

Even though she had enjoyed having sexual intercourse with Thomas during the first weeks of their marriage, Lola soon grew tired of his embraces. Over the following months, her romantic illusions were shattered, transforming her from an innocent girl of eighteen into a hardened young woman who had a low opinion of her drunken spouse.

She therefore had few qualms about betraying her wedding vows, and the first man with whom she committed adultery was Lord Normanby, the Lord-Lieutenant of Ireland, who was a notorious rake.

As was the custom among army officers, Lieutenant James presented his wife to the Lord-Lieutenant at a viceregal ball in Dublin Castle, and His Excellency was instantly spellbound by her beauty. He paid her many compliments during the evening, dancing with her several times.

A few days later, Lord Normanby summoned Lieutenant James and asked him to deliver some official documents to Army Headquarters in London.

"The courier I usually send has fallen ill," Normanby explained, "and I thought that, as you have no other duties while you are on furlough, you could perform the task in his stead."

"Sir, I would be glad to," replied James. "When do you want me to leave?"

"Right away," said His Excellency, handing over a sealed leather pouch, containing the documents. "After you deliver the pouch, I don't mind if you spend a couple of days in London before returning to Dublin. You could see some plays while you are there."

Lieutenant James boarded a boat from Dublin that afternoon, and the very next day, Lola received an invitation to have lunch with Lord Normanby in the viceregal lodge.

She, of course, accepted the invitation, but was a little surprised, when she arrived there, to find that she was the only person to be invited.

"Mrs. James," said Lord Normanby, welcoming her warmly, "I enjoyed talking to you on the night of the ball, and I would like to get to know you better— if you know what I mean. Do you have any objections?"

"No, not at all," she replied with a coquettish smile. "I can assure you that I know how to be discreet, and I shall never tell anyone about anything that might take place between us!"

"I am pleased that you understand me, Mrs. James, or may I call you Lola?"

"Yes, please do."

After they had eaten lunch, Lord Normanby took Lola upstairs to his private suite, ushering her into a large bedroom. A canopied bed was in the middle of the room, and in ten minutes the two of them were both naked and in bed together.

His Excellency fucked Lola three times before she left in the late afternoon. Two days later she received another invitation to visit the viceregal lodge.

Lieutenant James did not return from London for a whole week, and when he did, some of his fellow officers told him that they had seen his wife going into the viceregal lodge on at least two occasions.

The lieutenant's suspicions were aroused. He was aware of Lord Normanby's bad reputation, and he suspected that his wife had been unfaithful to him. He did not like being cuckolded and he was sure that the soldiers in the Dublin barracks must now be making lewd jokes about him.

Thomas James therefore decided to cut Lola off from the attractions of the viceregal lodge and the balls in Dublin Castle. He rented an old ramshackle farm-house in the country remote from Dublin, and abruptly told his wife that he intended to spend the remainder of his furlough there.

Lola was not at all pleased to receive such news. However, as she had no income of her own, she had no choice but to move with her husband to the dilapidated farm-house in the middle of the foggy boglands of Ireland. The following months were the most miserable and wretched of her life.

The lieutenant was absent from the house most of the time. He passed his days hunting foxes, and the evenings in the local tavern, drinking and gambling and fucking the rustic barmaids. He would return to the farmhouse late in the evenings in an inebriated state, and not get up out of bed until late the next morning.

Lola was seriously thinking of committing suicide when James was ordered to rejoin his regiment in India. She welcomed this news, because she had enjoyed her childhood years in India, and she had nothing but good memories of that country.

CHAPTER FOUR

Voyage to Calcutta

LIEUTENANT THOMAS JAMES and his wife sailed on the East Indiaman, *Blunt*, for Calcutta. The ship was loaded with a motley collection of passengers— officers, soldiers, missionaries, merchants, planters and prospective miners.

The lieutenant neglected his young wife during the voyage, and spent most of his time in the ship's smoking room, playing cards and drinking heavily. Finding the time heavy on her hands, Lola resorted to the commonest of all distractions on passenger ships—flirting. One of the men who fell under her spell was the captain of the ship.

Captain Joseph Higgins was forty years old, and he would often chat with her. Late one evening, she was on the deck of the ship, gazing up at the cloudless sky, when he approached her.

"Good evening, Mrs. James," he said. "It's a lovely moonlit night, isn't it? Where's your husband?"

"He's asleep in our cabin," she replied. "He had too much to drink, and he passed out. He won't wake up until morning."

This was the opportunity the captain had been waiting for. He already suspected that the marriage between Lieutenant James and his young wife was not a happy one, and he thought that she would not mind too much if he were to make advances at her.

"I hope you won't think me too forward if I pay you a small compliment," he said.

"I'm sure I won't. Please go right ahead."

"I think you are one of the most beautiful young ladies to ever board my boat, Mrs. James."

"You sure know how to flatter a young lady," she replied. "You are not trying to proposition me, are you?"

"Yes, I am. I hope you don't object."

"Not at all."

"In that case, Mrs. James, why don't we continue this conversation in my cabin? No one is likely to disturb us there."

"I would be glad to, but please, you must call me Lola. First names are so much more friendly, don't you think?"

"I certainly do, and you must call me Joseph."

The captain led Lola to his cabin, and as soon as the door had closed behind them, she threw herself into his arms, molding her slim body against his strong, muscular one.

The captain responded by kissing her long and hotly. Lola allowed her lips to open under his, and his tongue darted out, delving deep inside her mouth, their two tongues lashing together in lubricous delight.

Lola could feel the captain's swollen member pressing against her belly through their garments, and she rotated her hips against his, leaving him in no doubt that she welcomed his attentions.

"Would you like me to take off my clothes?" she asked, and without waiting for a reply, she immediately started to strip off her dress and undergarments, revealing her naked charms to the captain's admiring gaze.

He stared spellbound at Lola's unclad body, his burning eyes travelling from her uptilted breasts, down over her flat belly to the triangle of dark curls that adorned the juncture of her luscious thighs.

Lola twirled around in front of the captain, so that he could admire her nubile body from all angles. Glancing back cheekily over her shoulder, she wiggled her bottom from side to side, causing her admirer's upstanding cock to almost burst free of his straining fly.

The captain now ripped off his own clothes, throwing Lola onto the bed in the middle of the cabin, and falling forward on top of her.

"You little minx!" he cried. "I must have you!"

The captain fastened his lips to the jutting nipple of one of Lola's breasts, sucking avidly. He bit the nipple and lashed it with his tongue, causing her to sob with pleasure at the delicious contact.

"Oh, yes, that feels so good!" she moaned. "Now suck the other one! Oh, yes, yes, that's it! Oh, my God!"

Lola's breasts were soon tingling from the exquisite suction, sparks of desire shooting down from her saliva-covered nipples to her hot, oozing quim.

Her desires were now thoroughly aroused, and she placed her hands against the captain's shoulders, pushing downwards until his head was only inches away from her inflamed cleft.

"Lick my pussy!" she cried, and the captain happily obliged.

His tongue snaked out, delving between the slippery folds, searching for her swollen pleasure button. He licked and sucked with fervent eagerness, swallowing her delicious nectar.

Lola thrust her cunt up against his mouth, and he slid his hands under her rear end, his strong fingers squeezing the plump cheeks of her bottom. His tongue stabbed deep into her honeypot, and she gasped with delight, her hips bucking more and more wildly.

Lola could feel a mounting excitement building up within her loins, and she screamed out, "Quick, Joseph, stick your cock into my cunt!"

The captain instantly moved his body up over hers, ramming his shaft deep into her moist, slippery cleft.

Lola gasped happily as she felt his cockhead pressing against her cervix. After a few moments, he slowly withdrew his cock until only the engorged knob was between the clasping folds of her cleft, and then thrust it back into her once more.

"Oh, yes!" she moaned. "That's it! Fuck me with your big cock, Joseph! Fuck me, fuck me!"

The captain eagerly obeyed, ramming his cock in and out of her cunt. She gurgled happily, squeezing her vaginal muscles tightly around her lover's pounding shaft. The delicious pressure excited him to even more feverish efforts, the cabin resounding with their passionate gasps and screams of pleasure.

"Oh, yes, yes! I'm coming!! AARRGGGHHH!!!" gasped the captain as the spunk exploded from his cock, burst after burst filling her cunt to overflowing.

Lola welcomed his copious discharge with squeals of delight, her body jerking and flopping about as she was overwhelmed by one voluptuous spasm after another.

The two lovers now collapsed in each other's arms, resting for several minutes until they had recovered from their amorous exertions, and were ready to commence another course of pleasure.

When Lola returned to her own cabin, her husband was still fast asleep, and consequently, she did not have to explain what she had been doing for most of the evening.

During the rest of the voyage, Lola visited the captain several times in his cabin. As Lieutenant James was drunk most of the time, he never once suspected that his wife and the captain were lovers.

CHAPTER FIVE

Two Years of Misery

LOLA'S first year on her return to India was passed in the gay and fashionable city of Calcutta. Her husband was an obscure subaltern, but her father was the Adjutant General and this gave her entrée to the highest circles of Anglo-Indian society. She was warmly welcomed by the Viceroy and invited to all the official functions at Government House. As a result of her beauty and social graces, she was soon the acknowledged belle of Calcutta.

However, after the outbreak of the first Afghan War, she was torn away from the sparkling social life of the capital. Lieutenant James was posted to the military station at Karnal, a town between Delhi and Simla, which was a thousand miles from Calcutta, and Lola had no choice but to accompany her husband.

She spent the next two years in the lonely cantonment of Karnal, feeling trapped and wondering whether she would ever be able to escape from her abusive and dissolute husband. Fortunately, at the end of that time, she was freed from her husband as a result of an unexpected but most welcome occurrence.

An elderly British merchant, Samuel Smedley, and his wife had a large bungalow a few miles from the military post. Smedley was a very rich man, who owned a chain of stores dealing in British commodities throughout the Punjab. His wife was a young English woman, Dixie, whom he had married a few years earlier during a commercial trip to London. It was rumoured that this lady had agreed to marry the merchant in return for a substantial annuity.

Lieutenant James first met Dixie at a banquet thrown by Smedley. They were instantly attracted to each other. The lieutenant could be charming when it suited him, and he had already heard stories about Dixie's loose morals.

While they were chatting together, Dixie said, "I go for a horse ride early each morning, Thomas. Why don't you come over tomorrow morning and join me."

The lieutenant welcomed her suggestion, and the two of them soon got into the habit of going for early morning rides together before breakfast.

On one of these rides, Dixie suggested they should rest for a while in a glade beside a waterfall. When they had seated themselves under a shady tree, she said with an inviting smile—

"Well, Thomas, what shall we do to amuse ourselves while we're here?"

"Do you have something in mind?"

"Well, let's see. I'm a young lady and you're a man. Does that suggest anything?"

"Well, yes it does," replied Thomas with a grin, instantly seizing her slender body in his arms and kissing her.

When their lips parted, she said, "Let's take off our clothes. My husband hasn't made love to me for three months and I'm dying for a good fuck!"

James was more than willing to give Dixie the satisfaction she desired. In fact, he fucked her twice that morning before they rode back to her husband's bungalow.

Things went on like this for some weeks, and Smedley had not the least suspicion of his wife's infidelity. But then one morning the pair did not return from their ride. Smedley waited anxiously for two hours, and then sent some native servants out to look for them.

At about noon, Smedley rode to the Karnal military post in a highly agitated state. When he found Lola, he leapt from his horse, waving a letter in his hand.

"Read this!" he cried. "One of my servants just delivered it to me. My wife sent it from an outpost thirty miles away! She's run away with your husband! They've gone! What'll we do?"

Lola took the missive and read it:

"Farewell, you old fool! I'm sick of you. I'm off to the Nilgiri Hills with Lieutenant James. I am going with a man who knows how to give a woman the pleasure she craves, and I might add, he is glad to shake off a young wife who is too brainless to appreciate him. He says that he does not want to see her ever again!"

At first, Lola was stunned by the contents of the letter, and then she burst into wild laughter. She was at last free of her husband without her having to do a thing!

Lola returned to Calcutta and took refuge under her parents' roof. Her mother, however, was not pleased to see her, urging her to go back to England, and she finally decided on this course. Her father escorted her down to the harbour, and placed a cheque for a thousand pounds in her hand so that she would have some money to live on in London.

She stood on the ship's deck for some time as the vessel sailed down the Hugli river and out into the Bay of Bengal. She watched as the swampy shores of the coast receded from her across the waves, and at last went down to her cabin.

Many long years were to pass before she again saw India.

CHAPTER SIX

Divorce

THREE months later, Lola again set foot in London. She wanted a divorce from her husband, but in those days a wife could not sue for divorce. However, a husband could divorce his wife on the grounds of adultery. She therefore sought out some army officers who knew her husband and allowed them to enjoy her favours.

As the officers liked to boast of their conquests, word soon reached Lieutenant James in India that his wife had betrayed her marriage vows on numerous occasions. He was not slow to avail himself of the ample grounds she had provided for a divorce. He contacted a legal firm by mail and instituted a suit against her for divorce in the Consistory Court of London.

At the hearing of the case, a number of sworn affidavits from various witnesses were produced testifying to the defendant's misconduct over a number of months. The court was satisfied with the proofs presented to it, and pronounced a verdict of divorce *a mensâ et toro*.

With no understanding of the legal technicalities, Lola breathed a sigh of relief when she learned of the decision. She believed that she was free of her husband, but she was not. The decree was merely a legal separation, prohibiting the remarriage of either party so long as the other was alive.

CHAPTER SEVEN

Seeking a Career

LOLA GILBERT (who had reverted to using her maiden name) now sought a career. She realized that the money her father had given her would not last long, and she had no other means of supporting herself.

She was ambitious, and the only profession in early Victorian times that offered any promise for a young woman was the stage. She had read novels about girls who had become actresses, and the idea appealed to her.

She therefore took pains to acquire a knowledge of the Thespian art, and she studied under Miss Fanny Kelly, who was considered to be the most competent teacher of acting in London. In her heyday, she had been one of England's most gifted actresses, and she had retired from the theatre when about fifty to open a dramatic school for women.

However, despite all her efforts, Miss Kelly could not make an actress of her beautiful pupil.

"You will never, never master the art of acting," she told Lola sadly after three months.

"Is there no hope for me?" replied the distraught girl.

"For leading roles, I'm afraid not," said Miss Kelly, putting her arms about Lola. "You are possibly good enough to play minor roles on the stage, but you don't have the talent for great emotional acting. You could never play Juliet or Lady Macbeth."

"But what should I do now?"

"Have you thought of remarrying?"

"Yes, if I could hook a royal prince or a wealthy nobleman, but in the meantime I must have some source of income. "Oh, what will become of me?"

"Have you ever thought of becoming a dancer? You don't have to speak or memorize lines. You have a graceful, slender body, and I am sure you would be able to enthrall the male audience with your dancing."

"What sort of dancing do you think I should learn?"

Miss Kelly thought for some minutes. At last, she said, "Well, ballet is too stereotyped and con-ventional, and there is always the risk of damaging your toes while hopping about on them. Oriental dancing is too exotic and is disapproved of by the Lord Chamberlain. I would therefore suggest Spanish dancing, which offers opportunity for invention, variety and expression. At the moment, it is the most popular form of dancing in the major theatres of Europe, and if you are any good, you should have little trouble of obtaining engagements both here in England and abroad."

"In that case, I shall become a Spanish dancer."

"Splendid! If you are really serious, you must take a course of instruction under a Spanish dancer. Go to Spain! Go to the Pyrenees and Andalusia and study the dances of the gypsies and the peasants at the fiestas. I think it would be to your professional advantage to pass yourself off as a Spanish *danseuse*. English audiences like imported dancers. With your Spanish looks, you should be a great success!"

So in keeping with Miss Kelly's advice, Lola started to make preparations for a visit to Spain. She now assumed the name, Lola Montez, by which she was soon to be known throughout the capital cities of Europe.

CHAPTER EIGHT

First Stage Appearance

AFTER four months receiving instruction in Spanish dancing in Madrid, Lola returned to England, and Miss Kelly gave her an introduction to a theatrical manager.

Lola auditioned in front of Jasper Lincoln, the lessee of Her Majesty's Theatre in London, and her beauty and her dancing so impressed him, that he immediately engaged her to appear on his stage.

The morning papers of the following Saturday announced that, between the acts of *The Barber of Seville*, which was to be performed that evening, Donna Lola Montez of Madrid would make her first appearance in England, in a Spanish dance of her own creation, "El Olano".

On that evening, the theatre was crowded, and many titled and wealthy dignitaries were present. When the curtain rose between acts, a Moorish chamber was revealed. On either side stood a slave girl, gazing expectantly towards the draped entrance at the back of the stage. A moment later, the rear drapes were drawn aside and a figure enveloped in a mantilla glided onto the stage.

One of the slave girls snatched away the mantilla, revealing Lola in all her glory. She wore an embroidered satin bodice that clung to her jutting breasts, a short black velvet Spanish jacket gold-

37

braided at the shoulders, and a flamboyant skirt. In her raven hair, which cascaded down over her shoulders, was a red rose.

Clicking the castanets in her hands, she spun around in a pirouette and launched into a vivacious Andalusian dance, the lithely movements of her supple body beguiling the audience. Her lustrous eyes flashed, and her shapely hips swayed to the rhythmic music of the orchestra. Her sharp staccato laughter pealed through the theatre as her impassioned dance approached a crescendo.

She glided, soared and spun in a dizzy display of energy, and then with a final spinning pirouette, she collapsed to the floor, her head bowed and arms extended in a gesture of surrender.

After some seconds of silence, she leapt to her feet and bowed respectfully to the audience, who rewarded her with salvos of applause. From the gallery thundered a stamping of feet and cries for an encore; from the stalls came a loud clapping of hands; while from the private boxes bouquets of flowers were thrown onto the stage.

Lola's first performance on the London stage had been a great success. The dramatic critics in the newspapers the next morning were profuse in their praise of her performance, and Jasper Lincoln extended her engagement with the theatre for a full month.

CHAPTER NINE

Adventures in Warsaw

LOLA was intoxicated by her success as a *danseuse* on the London stage, and as she had the utmost confidence in her own artistic ability, she decided to seek engagements in the European capitals.

She danced at various theatres in Brussels, Dresden and Berlin to great applause, and then proceeded to Warsaw, the capital of Poland, where she performed at the Court Theatre.

Poland was under the rule of Russia at that time, and the Viceregent was Prince Ivan Paskevich, a cruel and ruthless tyrant who suppressed unrest by killing all those who dared to defy him. He was hated by the Poles who lived in constant fear of the Russian soldiers under Paskevich's command.

Lola Montez had been in Warsaw only a week when she attracted the attention of the Viceregent. He happened to attend the Court Theatre one evening, and he was instantly enraptured by the beautiful Spanish dancer.

The next morning, the Prince sent his aide-de-camp to the theatre with a letter for Lola. She ripped open the long, official envelope and read the letter.

She was puzzled by its contents, which were in Polish, and she consulted the Theatre Manager.

"What does it say?" she asked.

"His Highness conveys his high opinion of your dancing and welcomes you to Warsaw," replied the manager. "You are invited to an audience at the Royal Palace at eleven o'clock this morning."

"Why, that's only an hour away? Is His Highness in the habit of inviting dancers to visit him at such short notice?"

"His Highness is a great patron of the arts, and a connoisseur of beautiful women," replied the manager with a smile.

"Oh, he likes beautiful women, does he? Well, I shall not go!" Turning to face the aide, who was waiting for her answer, she said, "Tell your master that previous engagements prevent me from accepting his invitation."

"That is most unwise," gasped the theatre manager. "It is neither politic nor safe to refuse His Highness's invitation. He does not like to be crossed!"

"Not safe?" retorted Lola. "I am an English subject, and I am free to leave Poland whenever I choose. Paskevich dares not do anything to harm me."

"Maybe not, but please remember that I am a Polish subject and must continue to live here in Warsaw. If you give offence to His Highness, I might be held responsible for sponsoring you and be punished by imprisonment."

Lola was silent for a few moments. At last, she said to the aide, "Please convey to His Highness that Donna Montez accepts the honor of an audience with him."

The theatre manager hailed a cab for Lola, and a few minutes after eleven o'clock, she was deposited at the entrance to the Royal Palace. A *major-domo* escorted her through a maze of corridors and chambers to Prince Paskevich's private quarters.

She was shocked when she saw the Prince, whose cadaverous features were like those of some ghoul from the depths of Hell. He was wearing a general's uniform. His shoulders were adorned with epaulettes and his chest blazoned with gold braid and medals. He had a diamond-studded sword at his side.

Lola approached the Prince and curtsied.

"Welcome to Warsaw," he said, lifting her hand to his lips and kissing it. "I would like to express my personal admiration of your superb dancing."

"Your Highness is very kind," she replied.

"I would also like to reward you with some gift as a token of my admiration."

"I am rewarded enough if my talents give happiness to Your Highness," she murmured.

"No, I must insist," said Paskevich with a ghastly smile. "I would like to reward you by inviting you to stay in Warsaw as my honoured guest. You will be provided with a large mansion and servants. You will also receive an adequate annuity to enable you to pay all your expenses."

"You are most generous, but I must beg to decline Your Highness's offer. I shall stay in Warsaw only so long as the public demands me."

"So you wish to bargain, do you?" exclaimed the Prince. "What is your price?"

41

Lola shook her head. "I don't have a price," she said quietly.

"Every woman has a price. What if I were to add a villa in the country to my offer? Is that enough to satisfy you?"

"Your Highness, I am a dancer, seeking only praise and distinction from my art. Please, I would like to leave now."

"Very well, Donna, you may depart, but please reconsider my offer. It will be to your own advantage to accept it!"

Lola recognized the threatening tone in his voice, and she laughed. Wheeling about, she left His Highness's chamber, striding through the corridors and chambers of the palace until she reached the front entrance.

That afternoon, the Chief of the Warsaw Gendarmerie called upon the dancer.

"Donna Lola," he said, "I would like to have a word with you."

"What about?" she asked.

"His Highness, Prince Ivan, has informed me that you have offended him. That was most unwise of you. The favours of royalty cannot be rejected with impunity. However, he is willing to forgive you if you accept his generous offer."

"You mean if I agree to become his mistress?" retorted Lola. "I have no intention of doing any such thing. He is one of the most repulsive men I have ever met, and I would die rather than share my bed with that monster! Have I made myself clear?"

The police chief shook his fist angrily. "My dear young lady, you are a little fool! I have warned you! If you do not do as His Highness wishes, you will suffer for your impertinence!"

When Lola appeared at the theatre that night, her performance was greeted with salvos of applause, but amidst the applause, there was some hissing. The next night there was more hissing, and Lola suspected that the police chief was responsible.

On the third night, when she took the curtain call after her first dance, the hissing was even more pronounced. She was now certain that the hissing had been orchestrated by the police chief, but she ignored it, continuing her performance until the conclusion of her final dance.

She bowed to the clapping and cheering audience, but the applause was almost muffled by a swelling outburst of derisive hoots and derisive jeers.

Lola refused to be intimidated, however. She had no intention of fleeing from the stage to escape the taunts and jeers of a gang of hoodlums.

Striding down to the footlights, she held up her hand. "My friends!" she shouted. "I beg your attention!"

The applause and the hissing subsided, and she proceeded to address the audience.

"For three nights now, a small group of hoodlums have hissed my performance on stage. You have heard them again tonight, and you may wonder who has hired them to taunt and mock me. Well, I'll tell you. The Chief of the Warsaw Gendarmerie has hired them to intimidate me at the command of his master, Prince Ivan Paskevich. A few days ago, I was summoned to the Royal Palace, where that monstrous old man asked me to become his mistress. Well, I refused, and since then I have been hissed each night at this theatre."

Lola paused a moment to gather her breath, and then continued—

"His Highness thought he could buy my favours but I refused. There was no way I could ever accept riches and lands from a cruel tyrant who has ruthlessly oppressed the Polish people, torturing and executing all who oppose him. Even though I am a stranger in your kingdom, I sympathise completely with the citizens of Poland, and pray that some day you will rise up and free yourselves from the yoke of Russian rule!"

Without realizing it, Lola's impassioned words had an electrifying effect on the audience. They turned upon the hoodlums who had hissed her, punching and kicking the offenders until they fell to the floor. The audience then surged out into the street in front of the theatre, and it sounded as if a riot was breaking out.

Lola retreated to her dressing room to don her street clothes, and when she emerged from the stage door, she was greeted by a mighty cheer from the mob outside the theatre. The crowd had increased in numbers, the spirit of rebellion against their hated oppressors having been inflamed by the words of their heroine.

She hailed a cab, and an immense crowd of Poles, who hated the Russian oppressors, escorted her to her hotel, singing patriotic songs, and cheering loudly as she bowed and waved her hand at them.

In less than twenty-four hours, Warsaw was bubbling and raging with the signs of revolution. Marching crowds thronged the streets, but Prince Paskevich acted quickly to disperse the demonstrators. Troops of Russian cavalry and infantry, wielding sabres and firing guns, attacked the unarmed Poles, who were forced to flee or be slaughtered.

By the end of the day, more than three hundred rioters had been arrested, and order had been restored in the Polish capital. When she read the newspapers the next morning, Lola was horrified to discover that she was accused of being a spy and *agent provocateur* who had come to Poland under the guise of being a dancer in order to incite rebellion against the Muscovite government.

She was eating breakfast in her hotel room when a bellboy knocked on the door.

"Madame, half a dozen gendarmes are downstairs!" he gasped. "They have a warrant for your arrest!"

Lola immediately barricaded the door with a bed and some chairs, and proceeded to load the pistol that she had in her luggage. When the gendarmes arrived, they hammered on the door, and tried to force their way in.

"I'll shoot the first man who breaks into the room," shouted Lola. "I have a pistol and know how to use it!"

None of the gendarmes wanted to be the first to enter, and they went off to consult their superior officers.

An hour later, the Chief of the Gendarmerie arrived, and he told her that the arrest warrant had been waived, and replaced with an order for her expulsion from Poland.

"You are a fortunate lady," he said. "The British consul intervened on your behalf, and persuaded the Prince to allow you to leave Warsaw. You must depart within 24 hours."

After the police chief had left, the British consul visited Lola, and she thanked him for saving her from arrest.

"That's part of my job," he replied. "To rescue British citizens who get themselves into trouble when they are abroad. Where do you plan to go now? A coach is departing this afternoon for Berlin and another for St. Petersburg. I would suggest that you choose one of them before the Prince changes his mind about waiving the arrest warrant."

On the spur of the moment, Lola decided to go to St. Petersburg.

"Why do you want to go there?" asked the consul. "The Russian capital is almost seven hundred miles away. The journey there could take a week or more."

"I have heard that Czar Nicholas is a strong ruler, and I would like to meet him."

The consul laughed. "The Czar doesn't usually grant audiences to stage performers, but who knows? You are a very beautiful young lady, and he may be willing to grant you an audience. I will provide you with a letter of introduction to the Czar's aide-de-camp, Count de Benckenforff. When you arrive in St. Petersburg, show the letter to the Count, and he will,

I have no doubt, inform the Czar of your wish for an audience."

The Consul immediately wrote the letter of introduction and handed it to her, along with a bag of roubles.

"This is the payment for your performances at the Court Theatre," he explained. "Earlier today, I called on the theatre manager and demanded that he hand over the money owing to you. The money should be enough to cover the cost of your journey to St. Petersburg and hotel accommodation after you arrive there."

"You are very kind," replied Lola. "Your assistance is much appreciated.

CHAPTER TEN

The Czar of Russia

THE coach journey from Warsaw to St. Petersburg crossed the barren wastelands of Lithuania and the dark forests of Russia. In the middle of the journey, the storms of winter made it necessary for the passengers to change from the coach to a sleigh, but at last they reached the capital of Russia.

Lola presented herself to the Czar's aide-de-camp at the Imperial Palace, and after reading the letter of introduction, the Count said that he would speak to His Imperial Majesty, and let Lola know within a few days whether she had been granted an audience.

Two days later, the Count called upon her at her hotel.

"His Imperial Majesty has granted you an audience," he said. "I can tell you frankly that he has been informed of the trouble you created in Warsaw. His Majesty wishes to meet you, but I must warn you that he may decide to have you escorted to the frontier. You will soon know whether you are a welcome visitor to our country or not."

The audience was arranged for the next afternoon, and Lola arrived punctually at the Imperial Palace. The Count met her at the entrance and escorted her to the Czar's private apartment.

Czar Nicolas I was a commanding figure, tall and broad-shouldered. He had a high forehead, piercing eyes, aquiline nose and a strong jaw. He welcomed his guest warmly, shaking her hand.

"So you are the little firebrand who dared to defy Prince Paskevich," he said. "You are apparently unaware that, in inciting the Polish people to rise in rebellion against Russian rule, you committed a serious offence punishable by firing squad or exile to Siberia."

"From all that I have heard of Your Imperial Majesty's graciousness and kindness," she replied, "I am sure that you would not order the execution of a young lady like myself who was only seeking to champion the cause of a people who have been cruelly oppressed by Prince Paskevich."

There was a tense silence for several moments, and then the Czar's features softened.

"In your case, mademoiselle, I would never approve of the extreme penalty. I can appreciate the fact that you might have thought that you were doing the right thing. However, you cannot expect to get off scot-free. For the humiliation you inflicted on our viceregent, you shall suffer an appropriate and just punishment. Tell me, did you not feel some trepidation in placing yourself in my hands, the ruler of all Russia."

"No, why should I feel any fear of a sovereign who is famed for supreme gallantry, chivalrousness and honorableness towards women?"

A smile appeared on the Czar's face. "Mademoiselle," he said, "your case deserves grave consideration. I have not yet decided whether your offence is serious enough to deserve banishment. You will be informed of our decision in due course."

The Czar bowed. The audience was over.

A few days later, Count de Benckendorff called at Lola's hotel.

"I have come to deliver His Imperial Majesty's decision," said the Count, bowing formally and handing her a vellum envelope covered with elaborate seals.

Fearing the worst, Lola opened the envelope and read the Imperial edict. To her delighted surprise, she found that she was commanded to give a performance of her Spanish dances at the Imperial Palace.

She could scarcely believe her eyes. She had won the favour and patronage of the most powerful monarch in Europe and been invited to perform at the world's most magnificent court!

CHAPTER ELEVEN

A Dazzling Success

ON the momentous night appointed for her performance, Count de Benckendorff escorted Lola Montez into the ballroom of the Imperial Palace. The barbaric glare and glamor of the semi-Oriental court amazed her. Czar Nicholas and his consort, Czarina Alexandra, sat enthroned on a canopied dais above the assemblage of nobles, diplomats and military officers in colorful uniforms, and women in long gowns and sparkling jewelry.

Lola had never danced before such a grand audience, and she realized that, if she failed to impress the Imperial Court that evening, she would not be asked to give another performance, and she might just as well pack her bags and leave Russia right away.

Clicking castanets, she performed a wild, dizzy Andalusian dance unlike anything the audience had ever witnessed before, and her reception was rapturous. When her dance was finished, she was led to the dais where she was received by the Czar and Czarina.

At a signal, a court official came forward with an ornate jewel case. The Czar opened it and took out a necklace of flawless pearls.

"Mademoiselle Montez," he said, "we would like to present you with this tribute to your incredible artistic skill."

"Your Imperial Majesty is too generous," she replied, overcome with pride at being given such a gift by the Emperor of all Russia.

The Czar then presented Lola to the members of the imperial family and the Russian nobility.

During the giddy weeks that followed, she was invited to dinners and balls, and taken to roisterous parties in large log villas. She had innumerable admirers—princes and dashing blades of the nobility—who flocked around her, but she did not know that her admirers included Czar Nicolas until she received a summons to dine with him one evening.

CHAPTER TWELVE

A Night with the Czar

WHEN Lola arrived at the Imperial Palace on the appointed night, the Czar's aide-de-camp, Count De Benckendorff, was waiting for her at the front gate, and he led her through the palace to the Czar's private chamber.

Two uniformed guards armed with swords were stationed at the doors of the chamber, and they stood aside to allow the Count and the Czar's guest to enter the chamber.

After he had delivered Lola, the Count withdrew, closing the doors behind him.

Once they were alone together, the Czar did not waste any time with preliminaries, but immediately took Lola in his arms.

"My, my, you are a bold one," she murmured, placing her hands against the Czar's chest, making a show of mock resistance. "I don't recall that I gave you permission to embrace me."

"Dear lady, we both know why you are here. I think you are a very attractive lady, and I would like you to spend the night with me. You surely suspected what my intentions were before you entered my private chamber, so don't pretend otherwise."

"Well, maybe I did," Lola admitted. "I was just playing games with you, Your Majesty. I hope you did not think I was in earnest."

"No, I never once thought you might repulse my advances," laughed the Czar, enfolding the girl more tightly in his arms.

He kissed Lola on the lips, and she opened her mouth under his, allowing his tongue to delve inside. They kissed long and hotly, their tongues coiling and entwining together like two mating snakes.

When their lips parted, Lola asked, "By the way, where is the Czarina? Aren't you afraid that she might unexpectedly walk into this chamber and find the two of us together?"

"Not at all," replied the Czar. "We have separate chambers, and she would never enter my chamber without first asking my permission. Likewise, I would never enter her chamber without telling her in advance."

"Then we have nothing to fear. Would you like to help me out of my clothes?"

"Indeed I would."

In only a matter of moments, Lola's fur-lined coat and dress were lying in a crumpled heap on the floor, and her chemise and underdrawers quickly followed.

Lola was now completely naked, and she spun around in front of the Czar so that he could admire her body.

"Why don't you get undressed, too?" she suggested. "Or are you just going to stand there and look?"

The Czar instantly stripped off his royal garments, and Lola gasped in amazement when she saw the size of his fiercely erect cock. It was nine inches long and thick in proportion, standing up proudly from the base of his belly, twitching and jerking with lustful desire.

The sight of the Czar's prick caused Lola's pussy to tingle with eager anticipation. She had never been fucked by a royal monarch, and she could not wait to feel that long, thick shaft deep inside her cunt.

Nicholas now seized her in his arms, carrying her over to the large bed in the middle of the room and throwing her down on top of it. Lola sprawled out on the bed, her legs wide apart, exposing the crimson cleft between her legs.

The folds of her pussy were swollen and sopping wet with desire. She was yearning to be fucked by the Czar. All she could think about was his big cock!

The Russian monarch seized her ankles, pulling her legs even wider apart. His eyes burned with fierce desire as he admired Lola's inflamed cunt.

"What a lovely pussy you have!" he cried, his head plunging down between the actress's humid thighs.

The Czar's tongue darted out, licking the oozing folds of her cleft. He found her clitoris, teasing and titillating the swollen button. The voluptuous sensations produced by his lashing tongue were so exquisite that Lola was soon gasping and panting with delirious delight.

Great shudders of pleasure swept through her body, and her hips bucked wildly. She seized the back of the Czar's head in her hands, grinding her oozing pussy against his face.

"Oh, yes, yes! I'm about to come!!" she cried. "Oh—oh—oohhh!!!"

The Czar bit her clitoris sharply with his teeth, and the sudden erotic shock drove Lola over the edge. Her body went perfectly rigid for several seconds, and then shook violently as she was overwhelmed by one fierce spasm after another.

"Nicholas, you sure know how to eat pussy!" she murmured as the last tremors of her orgasm faded.

"I've had many mistresses and a lot of practice," the Czar replied with a laugh. "Now it's your turn to pleasure me, Lola. I want you to suck my cock!"

"All you have to do is ask," she replied.

The Czar stretched out on his back on the bed, and she knelt beside him. Leaning forward, she popped her red lips over the Nicholas's bloated glans, taking the swollen shaft deep into her mouth.

The Czar's hands played with her dark hair as Lola's head bobbed up and down, his gleaming shaft sliding in and out of her oral cavity.

"Oh, yes, that's it, you darling girl!" he gasped.

He could feel his orgasm approaching, and he gritted his teeth, sweat forming on his forehead as he tried to delay the final moment as long as possible. The voluptuous pleasure grew more and more acute until he could hold himself back no longer.

"Oh—oh—oohhh! I'm coming!! DRINK MY SPUNK, YOU DARLING GIRL!!!" he cried, his hips lifting up off the bed as he was overwhelmed by a violent orgasm.

Lola kept sucking the Czar's cock as his copious effusion flooded her mouth. She swallowed jet after jet of his jism, her throat muscles working rapidly as the warm, sticky fluid slithered down her gullet into her belly.

Finally, the Czar's cock stopped spurting, and Lola removed her mouth from the spent organ. She lifted her head, her pink tongue licking sticky strands of semen from her red lips.

"You're a great cocksucker!" said the Czar. "Now let's see if you can fuck just as good!"

The Czar seized Lola in his arms, rolling her over onto her back. The girl was pleased to see that the Czar's cock was still firmly erect, and more than capable of another orgasm.

Their naked bodies melted together, Lola welcoming his throbbing member with gasps of delight. She lifted her legs and wrapped them around his waist, locking her ankles together.

"Fuck me, Your Majesty!" she cried. "Fuck me!"

The Czar started to slide his cock in and out of Lola's slippery sheath, her hips bouncing up to meet each of his thrusts.

"Oh, yes, yes!" she gasped, running her hands down over his back. "Fuck me harder!! HARDER!!!"

Nicholas speeded up the pace of his strokes, the repeated impact of his pounding prick causing Lola's body to shudder and her plump breasts to wobble madly like two mounds of jelly.

The Czar was an incredibly virile man, and it did not take him long to gratify his lust. The voluptuous sensation in the tip of his cock grew more and more acute with each violent thrust of his long, thick shaft.

"Oh, yes, my dear!" he gasped. "This is it! AH—AH—AARRGGGHHH!!!"

The Czar spurted off in fierce spasms, his hot, sticky sperm filling Lola's cunt to overflowing. She arched her hips up under his, her body going rigid, and then jerking spasmodically as she was overwhelmed by her own crisis.

Her body thrashed and flopped about so violently that she almost dislodged the Czar's cock from her cleft. At last, however, her orgasmic tremors started to fade, and she unlocked her ankles, releasing her hold on Nicholas.

The Czar collapsed on top of Lola, gasping air into his heaving chest, but he did not withdraw his cock. It was still hard and rigid inside her belly, and after a few moments he resumed his long, deep strokes.

"Oohhh, I love a man who can keep it up!" cried Lola.

After they had enjoyed two more fucks, they fell asleep in each other's arms and did not awaken until morning when rays of sunlight slanted through the windows of the Imperial bedroom.

Lola had breakfast with the Czar, and before she left he gave her another present of expensive jewellery.

* * * * *

Under the patronage of His Imperial Majesty, Lola gave several more performances at court functions during her stay in Russia, and received

58

thousands of roubles in payment. She was soon in a very good financial position, and she had enough funds to protect her against the vagaries of fortune for some time to come.

As a result of her dazzling success at the Imperial Court, she began to dream of Paris, which was her artistic goal. She was sure that the prestige she had acquired in Russia would ensure that she would have absolutely no trouble in getting engagements in the theatres of the French capital.

CHAPTER THIRTEEN

True Love

LOLA MONTEZ waited until Spring, when the snows of Winter had all melted, before leaving Moscow for Paris. The distance between the two cities was more than one and a half thousand miles, and the long journey by coach took several weeks.

On arrival in Paris, she secured an engagement at the Opera Theatre, performing in *Il Lazzarone*, an opera by Halévy.

As in Moscow, she was a big success, and she was welcomed warmly by the somewhat Bohemian celebrities who frequented the Boulevard—the quarter between the Opera Theatre and the Rue Drouot.

The Boulevard—with its cafés and restaurants and theatres—was the accepted rallying point of authors and poets, painters and musicians, actors and journalists. By virtue of a selection which no one contested, nobody was tolerated there who could not lay claim to some sort of distinction or originality.

The headquarters of the noble company of the Boulevard was the famous *Café de Paris*, at the corner of the Rue Taitbout, and it was there that Lola met the French author, Alexandre Dumas.

The genial Creole was then in the prime of life, and had just reached the zenith of his fame with the publication of *The Three* Musketeers and *The Count of Monte Cristo.* He had a reputation as a libertine, and prided himself on the number of his conquests. He set his sights on Lola and invited her to spend a night with him in the large mansion he had built from the proceeds of his literary works.

Dumas was an accomplished lover, but it was clear that he considered their amorous encounter, enjoyable as it was, to be merely a one night stand. However, they continued to be close friends and often ran into each other in the cafés of the Boulevard.

Lola was chatting with Dumas in the *Café de Paris* one evening, when a young man entered the café.

"Ah, there's my good friend, Charles Dujarier," said Dumas, standing up and waving his hand. "Come over here, Charles. I would like to introduce you to Lola Montez. I think that the two of you have much in common."

Charles Dujarier was the editor of *La Presse* and a popular leader of the Republican Party.

"It is a pleasure to meet you, Mademoiselle Montez," he said, taking her hand and kissing it. "I have seen you perform several times at the Opera, and I was enthralled by both your beauty and your dancing."

"Flattery will get you everything," she replied with a seductive smile.

"I certainly hope so," laughed Charles.

Dumas was amused by the exchange between the two, and he could tell that they were attracted to each other. He therefore excused himself and wandered off to talk to friends at another table, leaving the two young persons alone.

Charles and Lola spent the evening in an enchanted world of their own, engaged in intimate conversation. When he took her in his arms and kissed her, she felt that she had at last found her one true love.

At the end of the evening, Charles offered to escort Lola to her hotel, and when they arrived there, she invited him up to her suite.

As soon as door was closed behind them, she made no pretence of maidenly virtue, but immediately stripped off her dress and under-garments, revealing her naked charms to Charles's admiring gaze.

Overcome by desire, he took a step forward, seizing Lola in his arms, covering her lips with his. They kissed passionately, their tongues darting into each other's mouths in erotic exploration.

When their lips parted, Charles lifted Lola in his arms, carrying her over to the bed and placing her down on top of the covers. She sprawled out on her back, her legs wide apart.

She smiled at him, sliding one hand down over her flat belly to the juncture of her thighs, her fingers parting the delicate pink petals. She inserted the fingers of her other hand between the moist folds and started to frig herself.

Charles stared spellbound at the lascivious spectacle, and was soon unable to remain a passive observer any longer. His eyes burning wildly, he climbed onto the bed, his face plunging down between her splayed thighs. He fastened his lips to her adorable pussy, sucking and licking eagerly.

Lola's own desires soon became aroused by his oral ministrations, and she arched her body, thrusting her hips upwards.

"Oh, my goodness, I'm almost there," she cried. "Quick, put your cock inside me, Charles. I'm about to come!"

Charles lifted his head from between her humid thighs, smiling down at the girl. He unbuttoned the fly of his breeches, pulling out his throbbing prick.

"Is this what you want?" he asked.

"Yes, yes! Quick, put it in me!"

Charles ripped off his clothes and knelt between Lola's spreadeagled legs.

She stared up at him, admiring his well-formed, athletic body. Smooth, round muscles rippled under his skin and his stomach was perfectly flat. His rigid weapon was the most impressive part of his anatomy, standing up straight and proud from the base of his belly.

He lowered his body onto hers, gradually sliding his prick into her cleft. Once his shaft was inside her up to the hilt, he did not immediately proceed to poke her, but instead lay perfectly still, allowing his swollen member to revel in the delicious warmth of her moist, clinging sheath.

Lola could feel his cock throbbing deep inside her belly, and she desperately longed for him to start thrusting it back and forth. She craved the pleasure which only the friction of a moving cock could give her.

"Oh, what are you waiting for?" she gasped. "Just don't lie there on top of me. Please do something. Fuck me with your big cock! Do it to me hard and fast!! FUCK ME!!!"

"Gladly," replied Charles, starting to move his cock in and out of her longing quim.

"Oh—oh—oh!" gasped Lola, swirling waves of passion lifting her higher and higher until she thought she could endure the delicious sensation no longer.

Charles spurted off deep inside her belly, and a moment later Lola spent profusely, the two of them writhing and swooning in rapturous delight.

When the last tremors of their mutual crisis had faded, Lola found that Charles still had his cock inside her, just as hard and rigid as before. Without withdrawing, he started to drive his cock in and out again, poking her steadily with long, leisurely strokes.

A feeling of extreme lassitude overcame them in the wake of their second amorous combat, and the two of them soon fell into a deep sleep.

Lola was awakened by the first rays of the morning sun slanting in through the windows of the hotel suite. Still half asleep, she rubbed her eyes, sitting up in the bed. Looking to one side, she saw that Charles was still fast asleep beside her.

She shook his shoulder, and when he awoke, she said, "I love you, Charles. You are the only man I have ever really loved. I will be heartbroken if you don't feel the same way about me."

"I love you, too," he replied. "I want to spend the rest of my life with you."

"Oh, I am so glad to hear you say that, Charles."

CHAPTER FOURTEEN

Invitation to a Party

CHARLES DUJARIER was a man of uncommon genius, and greatly loved and respected by all who knew him, except for those who disagreed with him in politics, and who dreaded the scorching and terrible power of his pen.

Dujarier spent almost every hour he could spare from his editorial duties with Lola Montez, and from him she rapidly acquired a knowledge of politics, and became a confirmed hater of tyranny and oppression, in whatever shape it came.

At Charles's suggestion, she studied books on political science, sociology, government and history, especially the doctrines espoused by American politicians such as Alexander Hamilton, Thomas Jefferson and Benjamin Franklin.

Lola soon acquired a knowledge of the state of politics throughout the major countries of Europe, and became so enthusiastic a Republican that she wished, in her heart, that she was a man, so that she could stand for election to high office and play a part in determining government policy.

The next two years were happy ones for the two lovers, but alas, the inscrutable hand of Providence was about to intervene and destroy that happiness!

Dujarier's newspaper, *La Presse,* championed the Republican cause, and its rival was the *Globe,* which was edited by Jean de Beauvallon, a staunch Royalist. As Charles was by far the better journalist, his paper had a much larger readership than the *Globe,* and de Beauvallon was desperate to find some way to silence the Republican paper.

Charles was not at all suspicious when he received an invitation from Mlle Fifi Liévenne to attend a supper party at the *Frères Provençaux,* a fashionable restaurant in the Palais Royal. The other invitees consisted mostly of minor actresses who were well known for their loose morals, while the men were rakes who enjoyed the company of such ladies.

Lola was also invited, but she chose not to attend, as she considered it beneath her dignity to attend such a party. However, as it promised to be a lively affair, she insisted that her lover go along and enjoy himself.

When Charles arrived at the restaurant, the party was in full swing. About two dozen guests were present, and he was welcomed warmly. To his surprise, Fifi Liévenne favoured him with her attentions, inviting him to sit beside her at the head of the dining table, and telling him that she had long admired his newspaper articles.

The merriment of the guests increased as the night progressed. Jokes, badinage and mockery flashed across the table, and the popping of corks from wine bottles was like a bombardment of miniature cannons.

Charles was not in the habit of drinking more than a few glasses, but as soon as his glass was drained,

Fifi would beckon the waiter. As a result, his glass was not allowed to remain empty, and Charles soon lost count of the amount of wine he had imbibed.

After a few hours, a number of new arrivals joined the party. They had come to dance and gamble, and the musicians struck up a minuet. The dining table was removed and some of the guests started to dance, while a card table was set up for the others.

As Charles was unsteady on his feet, he did not join the dancers. He thought that, in the midst of the revelry, he would be able to leave the restaurant unobtrusively and make his way back to his lodgings.

However, before he could reach the door, he was stopped by Jean de Beauvallon.

"Where are you going, Charles?" asked de Beauvallon, who seemed in a genial mood.

"Home. I think I'll call it a night," replied Charles.

"Why don't you stay and join us in a game of cards? After all, Mlle Fifi did throw this party in your honour. It would be most ungentlemanly if you left this early in the evening."

"I was not aware that the party was in my honour," laughed Charles, "although I did notice that Fifi has spent most of her time with me this evening. Maybe I could stay for another hour."

Monsieur de Ravin acted as banker at the table, and the cards were dealt. During the play, brandy was served freely and Charles lost more frequently than he won.

The candles burned low, and finally the party began to break up. Charles had lost a total of twenty-five louis.

As he was preparing to depart, Jean de Beauvallon and a couple of gentlemen approached him.

"Monsieur, before you go, don't you think we should square accounts?" said de Beauvallon.

"Square accounts? What do you mean?"

"You owe me fifty louis."

"For what, Monsieur?"

De Beauvallon's face twisted in an ugly leer. "You doubt my word?"

"I have no recollection of leaving anything unsettled with you."

"Are you accusing me of trying to cheat you?" snarled de Beauvallon. "That is an insult."

"I owe you nothing, you lying blackguard," replied Charles. "But rather than have these gentlemen think that you have any claim upon me, I will give you the money."

Unsteadily he drew out his purse and counted out the gold coins, tossing them in de Beauvallon's face.

"You are a scoundrel!" said Charles. "I didn't owe you any money, and now you can't claim that I do. I guess that settles accounts!"

"Settles accounts? Not by any means, Monsieur!" hissed de Beauvallon, and turning to the two gentlemen, he said, "You heard him, Messieurs. He called me a cheat!"

"Yes, we heard him malign you," they replied. "We can attest to that."

CHAPTER FIFTEEN

The Duel

THE next day, the Comte de Flers and the Vicomte d'Ecquevillez called upon Charles Dujarier at the office of *La Presse*.

"We have come on behalf of Monsieur Jean De Beauvallon," said the Comte. "Monsieur De Beauvallon considers himself insulted by your remarks last night and demands an apology or satisfaction."

"I don't apologise to cheats!" replied Dujarier.

"Then Monsieur de Beauvallon challenges you to a duel. If you don't accept, he will force you to fight—if necessary by a blow or an insult."

"I accept the challenge," replied Dujarier. "My two seconds will be Alexandre Dumas and Arthur Bertrand."

When Dujarier spoke with his seconds later that day, they were horrified.

"You have hardly ever handled a pistol or a sword in your life," exclaimed Dumas, "while de Beauvallon is an excellent swordsman and a deadly marksman with a pistol. He has already killed half-a-dozen men in duels. Tell me, what did you do to upset him?"

Dujarier recounted the events leading up to the challenge as far as he could remember.

"So that's what happened," reflected Dumas. "You were lured into a trap, Charles. Those harlots kept plying you with wine until you were dead drunk. They would have been well paid for their work by De Beauvallon. He then invited you to play cards, and he tricked you into calling him a cheat. There's no way you can avoid fighting the duel, if you don't want to be called a coward. Does Lola know?"

"No, she must not know. She would be worried sick if she knew that I was to fight a duel!"

"Inasmuch as you must face de Beauvallon, we must think of a way to avoid a fatal outcome. As the offended party, you have the choice of weapons. I suggest you choose pistols. De Beauvallon will certainly kill you in sword fight, but with a pistol there's always a chance. A pistol can slay an adversary, even if the trigger is pulled by some-one like yourself who is not a good shot."

On the morning of the duel, Charles scribbled a note to Lola:

"MY DARLING,—I am going out to fight a duel at ten o'clock this morning. I did not tell you before because I wished to spare you any worry. I will be with you at two o'clock, unless——

"Good-bye, Lola, the only girl I have ever loved.
"CHARLES."

It was seven o'clock, and he told his servant to deliver the letter about nine. He then rose and walked to Bertrand's house in the Rue Pinon, where he found the four seconds in consultation.

After the conditions of the encounter were signed and read, de Flers and d'Ecquevillez went in search of their principal.

Charles Dujarier and his friends drove to the Rue Laffitte, where they picked up a doctor, Monsieur de Guise, and all four then proceeded to the Bois de Boulogne.

The rendezvous was a secluded spot near the *Restaurant de Madrid*. The morning was intensely cold, and no one was about. A few snowflakes were falling as the party arrived. There was no sign of de Beauvallon and his seconds, though it was now ten o'clock.

Eventually, a cab drove up and out of it jumped de Beauvallon and his seconds. Dumas accosted de Beauvallon, remarking that it was confoundedly cold, and that Dujarier had been kept waiting for an hour and a half.

The combatants were placed at a distance of thirty paces from each other, and according to the conditions, each could take five steps forward before firing, but after one combatant had fired, the other must fire his own shot without advancing another step.

Charles Dujarier strode forward quickly, and at the end of five steps, extended his arm and aimed the pistol, pulling the trigger. The bullet hit de Beauvallon in the chest and he stumbled backwards.

However, the shot had evidently done little damage, for de Beauvallon was still on his feet. Swinging up his arm, he fired his own weapon and the bullet hit Dujarier in the forehead, killing him instantly.

A few seconds later, a coach pulled up and Lola jumped out. She had arrived too late to talk Dujarier out of fighting the duel, but not too late to see him fall to the ground. She rushed forward, throwing herself on the dead body of her lover.

Alexandre Dumas, Dujarier's second, now stepped forward. One thing puzzled him. Even though de Beauvallon had been shot in the chest, no blood had spurted out. There could only be one answer to explain the lack of blood!

"This man is a murderer!" said Dumas, pointing a finger at de Beauvallon. "The duel was not a fair fight. He must have been wearing mail armour under his shirt. Otherwise, he would have been wounded by Dujarier's bullet!"

"My God, you are right!" cried the doctor. "I saw the bullet hit de Beauvallon in the chest, but there's no blood."

"Of course, there isn't any blood!" scoffed de Beauvallon. "Dujarier's bullet didn't hit me. You are mistaken if you think it did. It missed me by a mile."

"No, it didn't miss you!" cried Dumas, knocking de Beauvallon to the ground and tearing open the latter's shirt to reveal a mesh of woven steel underneath. "Look, there's the bullet—imbedded in the steel mesh. The bullet would have pierced your heart but for the armour!"

The funeral of Charles Dujarier took place a couple of days later in the cemetery at Montmartre, and was attended with characteristic pomp. A flowery oration was delivered at the graveside by Alexandre Dumas.

Jean de Beauvallon was subsequently arrested and tried for murder, and among the witnesses were Alexandre Dumas and Lola Montez, who both swore on oath that de Beauvallon had been wearing mail armour under his shirt during the duel, and therefore had an unfair advantage over his opponent. As a result of this testimony, the court found de Beauvallon guilty of murder, and he was sentenced to death.

The execution took place one week later.

CHAPTER SIXTEEN

King Ludwig of Bavaria

AFTER the death of her lover, Lola Montez quitted Paris for Munich, the capital of Bavaria, where she hoped to secure an engagement.

On her arrival in that city, she immediately approached the director of the Royal Theatre, Herr Anton Richter, who agreed to view an exhibition of her dances. However, despite her well-known earlier successes in the other European capitals, Herr Richter told her that the dances did not meet his artistic requirements and that an engagement was out of the question.

Lola had no intention of allowing the director's decision to go unchallenged, and she appealed to Count Otto de Rechberg, the Chamberlain of the Royal Court.

"Herr Richter has refused to allow me to perform on the stage of the Royal Theatre," she complained.

"What reason did he give?" asked the Count.

"He told me that my dances are not suitable. I have danced before the Czar of Russia, and my performances were applauded by him. I do not understand why Herr Richter will not allow me to perform here in Bavaria."

"So that's the problem, is it?" said the Count with a laugh. "Herr Richter doesn't like Spanish dancing, and I suspect he has refused you on those grounds alone. I shall try to arrange an audience for you with His Majesty, so that you can tell him in person of your complaint."

Clapping her hands, Lola cried, "How can I ever thank you."

"I but serve His Majesty," replied the Count.

A few days later, he informed Lola that an audience with the King had been arranged.

On the appointed day, the Count met her at the palace gates and escorted her to the royal chamber.

His Majesty was seated upon a throne-like chair behind a large desk, both of which were located on a dais. Along the walls of the chamber were antique Greek and Roman statues on pedestals, and hanging on the walls behind the statues were paintings by some of Europe's most famous artists. On the desk there were numerous books, and His Majesty was jotting notes from an open volume.

When Lola was announced, the sovereign, who appeared to be in his sixties, rose to his feet. He was wearing a plain crimson jacket and looked more like a scholar than a king.

"Your Majesty, this is the Spanish dancer, Mademoiselle Lola Montez."

As she was familiar with court etiquette, Lola made a graceful bow of obeisance, and waited, with downcast eyes, for the king to address her.

"Mademoiselle, it is a pleasure to meet you," said His Majesty. "Your fame has preceded you. I have heard that you set both Moscow and Paris alive with your dancing. Not only are you a dancer, I can see

76

with my own eyes that you are one of the most beautiful women in all of Europe."

As he paid her this compliment, the king's eyes travelled in obvious admiration from Lola's face down to the low-cut bodice of her dress, which amply revealed the upper swells of her firm, jutting breasts.

"Your Majesty, I would like to thank you for granting me this audience," she said. "I hope you will pardon my intrusion upon your valuable time."

"You are in no way an intrusion. I am delighted to be visited by a young lady whose beauty exceeds that of the goddess Venus herself. Tell me, why have you requested this audience?"

"Sire, as you know, I am a dancer, and I have come to Munich seeking an engagement, but the Director of the Royal Theatre has refused to give me one. His whole manner was hostile, and I cannot understand why. As an artist seeking to pursue a career, I beg that Your Majesty grant that I be permitted to give performances here in Bavaria."

"You have my permission," replied the King, who was already bewitched by the beautiful dancer. "In fact, I shall issue an official command for you to appear at the Royal Theatre, and I will myself attend your *première!*"

Lola was delighted at the King's response. "Your Majesty is most kind."

"Mademoiselle, how could I possibly refuse the request of such a lovely lady? I trust your stay here in my city may be long and happy. With your consent, I shall immediately commission an artist to paint your portrait."

"Sire, you have my consent."

On Saturday evening, Lola performed her "native Spanish dances" at the Royal Theatre in the intervals between the three acts of the play, *The Enchanted Prince*, by J. von Plotz.

She was clothed in a Spanish costume of silk and lace, and she bowed before the King, who occupied the royal box. She then launched into her dance, riveting the attention of the audience. The sinuous swayings of her body expressed glowing passion, and then light-hearted playfulness, and the spell was not broken until she ceased her rhythmic movements.

To fully convey his admiration of her graceful dancing, King Ludwig invited Lola to a private audience on the Sunday morning following her performance.

They discussed the ancient Greek and Roman poets and the metaphysical philosophy of Socrates and Plato, and the King was amazed by Lola's familiarity with classic literature.

They chatted away happily and soon discovered that they were kindred spirits, not only as far as literature was concerned but also politics. Both believed that governments should serve the people, and that rebellion against tyrants was justified.

An hour passed without them realizing that time was flying.

Towards the end of the interview, the monarch asked, "Are you really Spanish, Mademoiselle?"

"Partly," she replied. "I am descended through my mother from Count Montalvo of Spain."

"Can you speak Spanish?"

"I have some knowledge of the language, Sire. I lived in Madrid for several months while I was studying Spanish dancing."

"Spain is a country I have long desired to visit," said the King, "but I cannot speak a word of Spanish. Would you be able to give me language lessons, Mademoiselle?"

Lola nodded her head. "My Spanish is not perfect, Sire, but I can teach you some common phrases that would allow you to communicate with the people."

"When will you be able to commence the lessons?" asked the monarch eagerly. "Tonight, Mademoiselle? Would that suit you?"

"Yes, it would," she said.

CHAPTER SEVENTEEN

In Bed with the King

LOLA suspected that King Ludwig's purpose in requesting her to come to the palace that evening had little to do with learning to speak the Spanish language, and she was right.

When they were seated, the King took her hand in his, squeezing it gently.

"You are a very attractive young lady," he said. "I hope you won't think me too forward if I kiss you."

"Not at all," Lola replied. "You are the King of Bavaria, and it would be wrong of me to take offence at anything Your Highness might say or do."

"Do you really mean that, my dear?"

"If I did not mean it, I would not say it," she replied with a mischievous smile. "You are free to do whatever you like with me."

The invitation in her words was too clear for there to be any mistake.

"Oh, you darling creature!" exclaimed the King, seizing her slender body in his arms, showering her with passionate kisses.

Lola voiced not one word of protest as the King's roaming hands pawed her breasts, freeing them from the bodice of her blue dress.

"What a lovely pair of bubbies!" he exclaimed, popping his lips over first one crimson nipple and then the other, sucking each until it had swollen into an elongated point.

Meanwhile, one of his hands was busy at work under her petticoats, feeling up between her legs. The hand soon reached the top of her white stockings.

"Oh—oh—oh!" moaned Lola as His Majesty's fingers found the opening of her drawers, slipping inside to fondle the moist slippery folds of her oozing quim.

"Do you like that, my dear?" the King enquired, inflaming Lola's desires with the rapid friction of his fingers.

"Oh, yes, yes, I do!" she cried. "Your Highness, you can make love to me if you want!"

Delighted by her response, the King lifted her in his arms, carrying her through into the adjoining bed chamber.

"Let's take off our clothes," he said, and they were soon both naked.

Lola fell backwards onto the bed, stretching out her arms to the King and he threw himself on top of her, ramming his royal cock deep into her warm, slippery cunt.

He fucked her with hard, fast strokes, and Lola lifted her hips to meet each of his thrusts. They were both eager to slake their burning desires, and they came within seconds of each other.

"Oh, yes, yes, this is it!" shouted the King, spurting off deep inside Lola's belly, and she welcomed his copious spend with squeals of delight, joining him in a glorious climax.

After the last tremors of their mutual orgasms had faded, they collapsed in each other's arms, sinking into the delicious lassitude of spent passion.

Several minutes passed before they recovered from their amorous exertions. The King's cock was still rigidly erect, and he fucked her another two times before they fell fast asleep.

The next morning, they had breakfast together, and they discussed politics. Lola had acquired a good knowledge of this subject as a result of her visits to the major countries of Europe, and His Majesty was most impressed by her accounts of her adventures in those countries.

Before Lola left to go back to her hotel, the King asked whether she would be willing to abandon her stage career.

"I would like to offer you a position as my adviser on political matters. You will receive a handsome salary. Would such a position interest you?"

Lola was silent for a few moments before replying. Dancing was a precarious profession, and in between engagements, she had often found herself short of money. She had little doubt that, as an adviser to the King, she would be paid much more than she could ever hope to earn as a dancer.

"Yes, Your Majesty, I accept your offer," she replied.

Lola performed only one more time at the Royal Theatre. At the conclusion of her last appearance, her enraptured audience accorded her a prolonged ringing ovation.

CHAPTER EIGHTEEN

The Uncrowned Queen

FIVE DAYS after her final performance as a professional dancer, Lola was formally received at the Royal Court.

King Ludwig and Queen Therese were seated on the dais of the magnificent throne room, which was thronged with courtiers and ladies-in-waiting, ministers and councillors and members of the diplomatic corps.

Lola Montez was a ravishing vision of beauty in her gown of white silk, and all eyes were fixed on her as she entered the large room where the aristocracy of Bavaria were assembled. The court herald announced her presence, and she advanced to the dais, respectfully making her obeisance.

King Ludwig smiled tenderly, presenting her to his Queen and then to his court and ministers.

"I would like to introduce Mademoiselle Lola Montez to the Royal Court," he said. "She is a descendant of the Count de Montalvo, and a close friend of Czar Nicholas of Russia. She has an extensive knowledge of European politics, and I have appointed her as my adviser. She will henceforth play an important part in all decisions affecting the governance of Bavaria."

84

The King's announcement was met with stunned silence by his ministers. They looked at each other, aghast at learning that a dancer of dubious morals was now an adviser to the King, and had the power to influence his decisions.

Who knew what she might do if not stopped!

Within only three months, the worst fears of the King's ministers were realized. The Ultramontane Party had long held power in Bavaria, largely because his Majesty had been willing to leave government in the hands of those capable of administration, while he had occupied himself with his studies of antiquity, the classical poets and the worship of Venus. But all this changed now that Lola had been installed as the king's adviser.

The first official expression of Lola's influence over King Ludwig was a Royal Decree transferring the control of the Department of Education and Public Worship from the hands of the Minister of the Interior, Karl von Abel, into those of the King's newly appointed adviser.

Karl von Abel was the Leader of the conservative Ultramontane Party, which was in league with the Jesuits, and with one stroke of the pen, the King had destroyed the control of von Abel and the Jesuits over the universities and schools.

Other measures followed quickly. Under Lola's counsels, a total revolution took place in the Bavarian system of government. The existing ministers, all members of the Ultramontane Party, were dismissed, and new and more liberal advisers were chosen. The power of the nobility and the Jesuits was broken, and the citizens of Bavaria were no longer subject to the autocratic rule of a small aristocratic and clerical elite.

The King approved of the reforms Lola had initiated, and he rewarded her for her political services. She was given the title of Countess of Landsfeld, accompanied by an estate of the same name, and an endowment of twenty thousand florins.

Karl von Abel and the Jesuits had no intention, however, of giving up without a fight. They were furious at being ousted from power by Lola. They considered her to be a fiend, possessed by demons, and they plotted ways to get rid of her.

They attacked her in the press, launching a campaign of scurrilous vilification and ridicule against her. She was described as a promiscuous harlot, a mercenary spy and an agent of the English Government which wanted to destroy the Catholic Church.

This campaign failed, however, and Karl von Abel decided that the only way to drive the Spanish she-devil out of Bavaria was to use physical force.

CHAPTER NINETEEN

Expelled from Bavaria

LOLA resided in a mansion of gleaming white marble which had been given to her by the King. The mansion was located on the outskirts of the city, and Karl von Abel paid a horde of hired thugs to attack it.

The attack took place one evening, when Lola was in the mansion. Night had already fallen when she heard the clamour of loud shouts. She went to one of the windows and looked out.

In the distance, she could see thousands of burning torches approaching along the road, and as they drew nearer, she saw that the torches were held in the hands of a mob of armed men.

The mob stopped in front of the mansion, the men shaking their fists and waving their weapons. Their eyes glowed like hellfire in the darkness. They were an ugly pack, the riff-raff and scum of the slums of Munich, snarling and growling, hissing and howling.

Lola was horrified to see a group of men placing a cannon in position opposite the mansion. Hundreds of the crowd were armed with muskets and pistols, and over a thousand more with swords, staves and axes.

A hired agitator was urging the crowd to smash open the doors of the mansion and swarm into the building.

"Down with the King's strumpet!" yelled the agitator. "Away with this Whore of Babylon, who cohabits with demons! Let her be driven forth! and her house of sin be burned to the ground! Out with the fornicating bitch! Stone her to death!"

The horde charged forward, some of them battering the doors of the mansion with their gun-butts, while others, armed with clubs and swords, smashed the panes of the iron-grilled windows of the lower floor. A fusillade of musketry tattooed the marble walls of the mansion, pockmarking them with bullet holes.

At this juncture, Count Otto de Rechberg arrived on the scene. He was on horseback, and saw the mob in front of the mansion. He rode through the melee on his charger, slashing at the enraged multitude with his sword. Cutting down all who tried to bar his way, he galloped around to the rear exit, which the attackers had not yet discovered.

The rear door was opened by a maidservant, who recognized the Count. He rushed upstairs to Lola's boudoir, and saw that she was about to step out onto the balcony to address the crowd.

"What are you doing, you foolish woman?" he cried, seizing her in his arms, and dragging her back into the boudoir and closing the window, just seconds before the cannon on the other side of the street roared.

The cannon ball shattered the glass window of the boudoir, missing Lola by only inches. The ball sped across the room, smashing a hole in the far wall.

"You must get out!" cried the Count. "The Army has sided with Karl von Abel, and is refusing to disperse the rabble. The Ultramontane Party has issued the King with an ultimatum, telling him that, if he doesn't expel you from Bavaria, they will remove him from the royal throne by force. For the King's sake, as well as for your own safety, you must flee from here at once."

Stunned by the Count's announcement, Lola looked about her in disbelieving bewilderment.

"But what does the King say?" she asked.

"His Majesty has no choice but to comply with the Ultramontane Party's demand if he wants to retain his throne. He has instructed me to advise you to disguise yourself as a peasant girl and escape into the country on foot. Go to the village of Weinsberg, and ask the Mayor for protection. His Majesty has already despatched a message to the Mayor, ordering him to offer you shelter. Your presence there will not be suspected and you will be safe until the present troubles are over. You will then be able to make your way to some other country where you can resume your career as a dancer."

Lola was silent for several minutes as she considered what she should do. She was tempted to stay and defy the mob who wanted to kill her, thinking it was better to die bravely rather than flee from her enemies.

"Madame, come at once!" cried the Count urgently. "There is not a moment to lose! The doors of the mansion have been broken down, and the east wing is on fire!"

At last, Lola gave in, allowing the Count to lead her out through the rear exit of the mansion, and along a lane towards the outskirts of the city.

At last, they reached the open countryside, and climbing to the top of a hill, she looked backwards and saw that the whole of the mansion was now afire, the lurid flames leaping upwards into the night sky.

CHAPTER TWENTY

Accused of Bigamy

LOLA MONTEZ had been driven from Bavaria without any hope of ever returning. There was no alternative but to seek shelter within some friendly state. She fled to Switzerland, but she was unable to secure an engagement there, so she went back to England.

On arriving in London, she went to see Jasper Lincoln, the lessee of Her Majesty's Theatre, and he offered her the lead role in a musical comedy *The Belle of Bristol*. The advertisements for the play billed her as "Lola Montez, Countess of Landsfeld", and the play attracted large audiences, as her activities in Bavaria were well known to the English public from newspaper reports.

After the show each night, young gentlemen would send flowers to her dressing room, along with notes inviting her to have supper with them, and she would frequently accept these invitations and sometimes allow the gentlemen to sleep with her.

Among her many admirers was Mr. George Trafford Heald, son of a rich Chancery barrister, and a cornet in the Second Life Guards. He was a tall young man, with boyish features, light brown hair and neatly trimmed moustache. He was about ten years younger than Lola, and did not appear to be too intelligent. However, he had just turned twenty-one and had inherited a large fortune from which the income was about ten thousand pounds per annum. He was accordingly considered by Lola to be a very good catch.

She was pleased to have so eligible a suitor, and when he proposed to her, in shy stammering words, she consented to be his wife. She did not feel any great affection for Arthur, but considered that it was to her advantage to have a rich husband.

She married George Heald at St. George's Church, Hanover Square, and as she left the church on the arm of her youthful husband, she thought that she could now abandon her stage career. She looked forward with complacency to a life of respectability and affluence as George's wife.

Things did not go the way Lola hoped, however!

Her new husband had a maiden aunt, Miss Suzanna Heald, who did not approve of her nephew's marriage and considered his bride to be a gold digger. Miss Heald therefore hired a private detective to investigate Lola's past, and the aunt was shocked when the detective informed her that Lola already had a husband from an earlier marriage.

George's maiden aunt wasted no time in taking legal action against Lola Montez.

The honeymoon of the newly wed couple was brief. Just one week after the wedding, at nine o'clock in the morning, there was a knock on the door of Lola's lodgings in Halfmoon Street.

When she opened the door, she found a large, strongly built gentleman standing on the front porch. He introduced himself as Police Inspector Whall, and requested a word or two with her.

"About what?" she demanded.

"I have a warrant for your arrest on a charge of bigamy?" said Whall.

"What are you talking about?"

"We have received information that your recent marriage to Cornet George Heald is illegal, because your lawful husband, Captain Thomas James is still alive."

"You are mistaken. Captain Thomas James is not my lawful husband. I was divorced from him by an Act of Parliament many years ago."

"No, you weren't. You are still married to Captain James. I must insist that you accompany me to the police station."

"Like hell I will!" retorted Lola, trying to slam shut the door of her lodgings, but the Police Inspector stuck his foot out to prevent the door from closing.

The Inspector was accompanied by a Sergeant, and they proceeded to seize Lola by the arms. She struggled to free herself from their grasp, but she was not strong enough.

They took her to the Marlborough Street police station, where she was formally charged, and from there she was taken to the police court at half-past one o'clock in the afternoon. The rumour of her arrest had spread abroad by then, and the approaches to the court were thronged with newspaper reporters.

Lola Montez was placed on a seat in front of the bar, and George Heald was allowed to have a chair beside her. She appeared quite unembarrassed, and smiled several times at the members of the press. She was stated to be twenty-four years of age on the police sheet, but she was, in fact, thirty-one.

Her reputed husband, during the whole of the proceedings, sat with Lola's hand clasped in both of his own, occasionally giving it a little squeeze.

After the presiding magistrate had taken his seat, the prosecuting counsel, Mr. Clarkson, opened the case against the accused. He stated that Lola had been married to Thomas James in Ireland, in July 1837, and that a judicial separation had been granted by the Consistory Court five years later. However, this did not constitute an official divorce, and Captain James was believed to be still alive in India.

The prosecuting counsel further stated that he was acting on behalf of George's aunt, Miss Heald, without the consent of her nephew, who would, if he could, prevent these proceedings. The counsel's application was for the accused to be remanded in custody until he could get witnesses from India to come forward.

Miss Heald, who went into the witness-box, explained her relationship to George Heald. She said she had been his guardian until he came of age and she considered it was her duty to prosecute this enquiry.

Mr. Bodkin appeared on behalf of the accused, and he pointed out that Lola had been dragged that morning to a police station to answer a charge which, in all his professional experience, was perfectly unparalleled. He could not recollect a case of bigamy in which neither the first nor the second husband came forward in the character of a complaining party.

The matter would, however, require investigation, and Mr. Bodkin was willing to concede that enough information had been laid before the court to justify further enquiry. At the proper time, he expected that he would be able to show that the accused's marriage with Mr. Heald was a lawful act.

He pointed out that the accused honestly believed that a divorce bill had been obtained in the House of Lords, and she had not deliberately broken the law. He asked the magistrate to release Lola on bail, and after a short consultation with the prosecuting counsel, the magistrate agreed to do so on payment of a surety of £1,000.

Bail was immediately tendered, and Lola and her husband were allowed to leave the court. Once they had returned to her lodgings, Lola said—

"George, I think it is likely that your aunt will be able to produce Captain James in Court, and I will be found guilty of bigamy. I really believed that I had been granted a divorce by the Consistory Court, but it appears that I was mistaken. If I am convicted of bigamy, I will be sentenced to several years imprisonment. I therefore suggest that we depart tomorrow morning for the continent, where I will be safe from arrest."

George, who was madly in love with Lola, agreed with her suggestion, and they boarded a ferry from Folkestone to Boulogne in France the next morning.

CHAPTER TWENTY-ONE

An Unhappy Couple

THE newly married couple proceeded in the first instance to Spain, and despite their pledges of affection, the domestic life of the Healds was soon troubled by violent quarrels, for there was a fundamental difference in their temperaments.

Lola liked to carouse in bars and gambling houses until all hours of the night, while George preferred a quieter and more sedate life. At Barcelona, he forbade his wife from going out at night without him, and when she disobeyed him, he slapped her across the face. In an access of fury, Lola stabbed her husband with a stiletto.

The wounded man took to flight, but unable to stifle his love for his wife, he returned to her with assurances of renewed affection. However, he soon found reason to regret this step, and at Madrid he again deserted the conjugal roof. Lola advertised for him as if he were a lost dog, and rewarded the person who found and restored him to her.

The pair wandered through Europe, and at last found themselves in the French capital. By now, Lola had firmly established her dominance over her browbeaten husband. He had begun to drink heavily, but she did not care that he was intoxicated most of the time, just so long as he continued to provide her with a regular allowance so that she could live a life of leisure and luxury.

CHAPTER TWENTY-TWO

A Lady of Pleasure

WHILE they were in Paris, Lola made another attempt to stab her husband, and this time he left her for good. He returned to London, without leaving her with any money to support herself. She therefore had no choice but to go the rounds of the theatres, hoping to obtain a role in some theatrical production. Unfortunately, no stage work was available at that time.

At this juncture in her career, she made the acquaintance of a French prostitute called Celeste Mogador, and when she explained her predicament to Celeste, the latter offered to help Lola.

Celeste said that she was acquainted with a pimp who found clients for her, and she was sure that he would be willing to perform the same service for Lola.

"His name is Auguste Papon, and he is a very discreet young man," Celeste explained. "The clients provided by him all come from the upper ranks of society—young aristocrats, lawyers, government servants, military officers and wealthy merchants. I pay him a ten percent commission for each client. If you like, I'll introduce you to him. What do you say?"

"I would definitely like to meet him," replied Lola. "I need the money. When will you be able to introduce me?"

"What about tomorrow? I suggest the three of us meet at noon in the *Café de Paris*. Does that suit you?"

"Yes, it does. I look forward to meeting Monsieur Papon."

The next day they all met as planned, and Auguste Papon agreed to act as a pimp for Lola. He asked for the address of the lodgings where she was staying, so that he could easily contact her when he needed to.

Lola returned to her lodgings, and early that evening Papon knocked on the door of her room.

"Would you like to come with me?" he said. "I told a young gentleman that I could introduce him to one of the most beautiful women in Paris, and he said that he would like to meet you. His name is Eugene, and he will pay you well if you please him."

Papon escorted Lola to an expensive hotel, and took her upstairs to the client's suite. Papon insisted that Eugene pay in advance for Lola's services, and then left them.

"Would you like something to drink?" Eugene asked when they were alone together.

"A glass of wine would be nice," she replied.

Eugene uncorked a bottle, and filled two glasses, inviting her to sit beside him on a sofa. After they had talked for a while, Eugene took her in his arms, kissing her on the lips.

"Would you like me to take off my clothes?" she said when their lips parted.

"Please do," replied Eugene.

She removed her garments one by one, revealing her flawless body to the young man's admiring gaze.

"Do you like what you see?" she asked.

"You know I do," replied Eugene, eagerly discarding his own clothes.

When they were both naked, she stretched out on the bed, and Eugene mounted her. He rammed his cock into her up to the hilt, fucking her in a wild frenzy.

"Oh, oh, oh, this is it!! I'M CUMMINGGG!!!" gasped Eugene as he spurted off, inundating Lola's cunt with burst after burst of hot, sticky spunk.

She came a few seconds later, and after the last tremors of their crisis had faded, they collapsed weakly in each other's arms.

One fuck was not enough to satisfy Eugene, however. After only five minutes, he recovered from his amorous exertions and was eager to run another course of pleasure.

"How would you like to do it this time?" Lola asked. "Would you like me to get on top?"

"Yes, let's do it that way," Eugene replied, stretching out on his back.

Lola swung a leg of his body, straddling his hips. Leaning forward, she sank down, engulfing Eugene's upright member within her clasping sheath. She tightened and relaxed her vaginal muscles, rotating her hips as she worked her slippery pussy up and down his iron-hard shaft.

"Oh, yes, yes!" gasped Eugene. "That feels so good!"

Lola sped up the pace of her movements, and they soon melted in another rapturous spend.

Eugene had already paid in advance for the session, but before he left he gave her an additional tip in appreciation of her services.

"You sure know how to pleasure a man," he said. "You're the best fuck I've had in a long time."

CHAPTER TWENTY-THREE

A Violent Client

OVER the next two weeks, Lola was fucked by more than two dozen clients, most of whom were well-behaved and did not give her any trouble. However, one client who was an exception was Colonel Lucio Borselli, a military attache at the Italian Embassy.

The colonel was about fifty years old with brutish features, bloodshot eyes and walrus moustache. As usual, Papon escorted Lola to the client's place of abode and collected payment from him before leaving her with the client.

When Lola first saw the Italian, she was shocked by his vulgar appearance, but as Borselli had already paid for her services, she had no choice but to allow him to enjoy her favours.

Lola stretched out naked on a large bed, and the colonel mounted her. His cock was too big to fit easily into her sheath, however, and she screamed out in pain. The colonel ignored her cries, his lips curving in a vicious smile.

He fucked her with hard, savage strokes and it did not take him long to complete the job. His body went suddenly rigid over hers, and a moment later, he spurted off, flooding the inmost recesses of Lola's cunt with his sizzling spunk.

"Did you enjoy that?" he asked with a malicious grin.

Lola, who wanted to avoid angering the colonel, thought it was best not to tell the truth.

"Y-yes, I enjoyed it very much," she replied. "I always like being fucked by big, strong men."

"I'm glad to hear that," said. "Well, the fun's not over yet. I want you to suck my cock."

He dragged her from the bed and made her kneel in front of him. Holding her head firmly in his strong hands, he forced the mushroom-shaped knob of his cock between her lips with one savage thrust.

"Take that, you bitch!" he cried as he started to work his shaft in and out of her oral cavity, battering the back of her throat each time he lunged forward.

Lola sobbed helplessly. The colonel's sinewy talons were entangled in her hair, and there was no way she could escape.

Borselli gasped and moaned, his muscular body quivering as his excitement mounted. Lola could feel his cock pulsing inside her mouth, and she knew that he was about to ejaculate.

"OH, YES, YES! I'M CUMMINGGG!!!" the colonel shouted loudly as the spunk exploded from his cock.

Borselli's orgasm seemed to last forever, but eventually he released his hold on her head, allowing her to collapse on the floor.

Lola hoped that her ordeal was now over, but she soon learned she was mistaken.

"Get on your hands and knees!" ordered Borselli. "I want to fuck your asshole!"

Lola had never been sodomized before, but she knew that she had no choice but to obey the brutal colonel's order. When she was on all fours, Borselli placed his rough hands on her shoulders, forcing the upper part of her body down, so that her face was pressing against the carpeted floor. In this position, her bottom was sticking up into the air, the puckered ring of her asshole clearly visible between her splayed buttocks.

Lola sobbed as the colonel forced his big cock into her tightly clenched anus. He had not bothered to lubricate her rear passage first, and the burning sensation of his invading shaft was almost more than she could bear.

Borselli lunged again and again, driving his cock deeper and deeper until its whole length was engulfed in the warm depths of Lola's rectum. Once he had succeeded in fully penetrating her, the colonel rested a few moments before starting to work his shaft back and forth within the delicious tightness of her anal passage.

Each stroke caused Lola to sob and whimper, but the colonel was merciless. He kept buggering her until he spurted off, flooding her bowels with burst after burst of sperm.

Lola's body now collapsed, and she sprawled out on her belly with the colonel's body on top of hers, neither of them moving for some minutes.

At last, Borselli climbed to his feet, and put his clothes back on.

"Well, that was good fun," he said. "I always enjoy fucking a girl in all three orifices!"

* * * * *

Afterwards, Lola told Auguste Papon about the Borselli's brutal treatment of herself, and he was shocked by her account.

"I'll make sure that he never treats one of my girls like that ever again," said the pimp.

Two days later, the Paris newspapers reported that the dead body of the Italian military attache had been found floating in the River Seine. The corpse had a bullet-hole in the back of the head!

CHAPTER TWENTY-FOUR

A Thrilling Threesome

A couple of weeks after the above incident, Auguste Papon told Lola that he had a client who wanted to have sex with two girls at the one time.

"You and Celeste Mogador get on well together," he said. "I thought that the two of you might like to entertain the client. What do you say?"

"Sure," replied Lola. "A threesome sounds like fun."

As usual, Papon escorted the two prostitutes to the client's hotel, collected payment from the client and then left.

On this occasion, the client was an English nobleman, Sir Percy Colman, who was visiting Paris, and he welcomed the two girls warmly.

After he had engaged in conversation with them for about half an hour, he suggested that they all take off their clothes.

When they had undressed, Lola slipped into Sir Percy's arms, kissing him long and hotly. When their lips parted, she stepped back, allowing Celeste to also kiss him.

Sir Percy's cock was soon standing to full attention. Although he planned to fuck both of these desirable females before the night was over, he wanted to amuse himself first by watching them pleasure each other.

"All right, girls, has either of you ever made love to another girl?"

"No," said Lola. "I'm not a lesbian."

"Nor am I," added Celeste. "I like men, not other women."

"Well, tonight, I want you to expand your sexual horizons. I enjoy watching two girls having sex with each other, and I'll pay you well."

"How much will you pay us?" asked Lola.

Sir Percy named a surprisingly large sum of money, and the two girls looked at each other. Lola nodded her head, and Celeste did likewise.

Lola then took her friend in her arms, kissing her on the lips, the two of them falling onto the bed together.

Sir Percy watched with spellbound fascination as Celeste stretched out on her back, and Lola positioned herself between her friend's widespread legs.

Lola fastened her lips to Celeste's cleft, her agile tongue darting out, delving deep into the moist, slippery folds. Lola licked and sucked the other's swollen love button with passionate zeal, causing Celeste to sigh and moan with mounting excitement.

The lascivious spectacle that was being enacted before his eyes made Sir Percy's cock twitch and jerk with uncontrollable desire. He could see the pouting lips of Lola's pussy peeping out cheekily from between the backs of her thighs, and he moved forward, climbing onto the bed behind her.

Sir Percy seized Lola's hips firmly in his hands and pressed his empurpled glans against the folds of her quim, forcing his cock deep into her sheath. Lola continued to gamahuche Celeste as Sir Percy shoved his cock in and out of Lola's pussy.

The young Englishman was in such a state of excitement that he came almost at once, his spunk spurting out deep inside Lola's cunt. The force of his spermatic outpouring triggered Lola's own crisis and she came a few seconds later. She lifted her head from between Celeste's thighs and arched her back, her petite body jerking convulsively.

When Lola's climactic spasms had faded, she applied her lips to Celeste's quim once more, while Sir Percy collapsed on the bed beside the two girls. Lola kept licking Celeste's cleft until the latter spent profusely, her squirting juices bedewing her friend's mouth and cheeks.

Sir Percy now told Celeste to pleasure Lola in the same way. Lola rolled over onto her back, and Celeste's tongue was soon working away between her friend's thighs. Sir Percy's sperm was oozing from Lola's quim, and Celeste licked and swallowed the sweet nectar.

Sir Percy watched this wanton exhibition with riveted eyes, and he soon had another cockstand. Celeste's head was down between Lola's thighs, her luscious bottom sticking up high in the air. The English nobleman rammed his cock into Celeste's cunt, poking her with long, deep strokes.

The bedroom soon resounded with a soaring crescendo of gasps and moans of pleasure as Celeste licked Lola's pussy and Sir Percy fucked Celeste's cunt. Before long, their rapturous excitement was too much to be endured.

Lola came first. Placing her hands against the back of Celeste's head, she thrust her hips up from the bed as her body was wracked by one delicious spasm after another. Celeste achieved her own climax a few seconds later, her body sprawling out on top of the Lola's.

When Celeste fell forward, Sir Percy's cock was dislodged from her cunt, and he knelt over the two girls, clasping his throbbing shaft in his hand and jacking off furiously.

"Okay, girls, this is it!" he gasped as long strands of white, sticky fluid exploded from his bloated knob.

Lola and Celeste opened their mouths to receive Sir Percy's liquid tribute. They swallowed every delicious drop of his spurting spunk before the three of them collapsed together on the bed.

After a short rest, they resumed their amorous sport, enjoying several more bouts of pleasure over the next few hours.

When the two girls left Sir Percy's hotel suite the next morning, he kept his promise by giving each of them a generous tip.

CHAPTER TWENTY-FIVE

America

SOON after the above session, good fortune favored Lola. She was dining in the *Café de Paris* one night, when she happened to meet an American theatrical agent, Edward Willis, who offered her an engagement in New York. Needless to say, she eagerly accepted the offer.

Lola sailed in the *Britannia* from Southampton to New York, where she was promptly surrounded by swarms of newspaper reporters as soon as she got off the ship.

A month after her arrival, she appeared in the title role of *Lola Montez in Bavaria*, a play that had been especially written for her. The play was performed at the Broadway Theatre, and ran for three months.

After her successful engagement in New York, she embarked on a triumphant tour of Philadephia, Boston, Washington and New Orleans. She attracted large audiences wherever she performed, and she was confident that she would have even greater success on the West coast of America.

She boarded a boat from New Orleans, crossing the Gulf of Mexico to San Juan del Norte. From there she took the land route across the Isthmus of Panama, and then boarded another boat up the Pacific coast to San Franciso.

Within a week of her arrival in San Francisco, she secured an engagement at the American Theatre, and it was there that she first performed her notorious Spider Dance, teasing her mostly male audience with tantalizing glimpses of her naked body.

Lola wore a Spanish costume for the dance, and the music was at first slow as she pretended to have become entangled in a spider's web. As she struggled to free herself, she was bitten by an imaginary spider.

The orchestra then began playing more lively music as she searched for the spider, lifting her petticoats and attempting to shake it loose. As the dance progressed, she exposed more and more of her legs, and at last pulled the petticoats up about her waist, revealing that she was wearing no drawers underneath.

She allowed the audience to stare at her exposed lower limbs for several seconds before shaking her petticoats and dislodging the imaginary spider. She stamped on the poisonous creature as the music reached a crescendo. The mostly male members of the audience left her in no doubt that they had enjoyed her performance. They cheered and shouted for an encore.

Lola obliged by discovering other imaginary spiders in her petticoats, the audience clapping and urging her to display even more of her naked charms. Her dance became more and more abandoned, and ended with her finding a spider in the bodice of her dress, which resulted in her baring her breasts as she sought to shake the creature loose.

The tumultuous applause of the male spectators was even more deafening than before.

* * * * *

Shortly before her arrival in San Francisco, gold had been discovered in California, and it swarmed with gold-seekers. After her success in San Francisco, Lola went on a tour of the mining camps, performing in the jerry-built saloons and dance halls which had sprung up almost overnight. In all of the camps, the miners always demanded that she perform the Spider Dance, and she never refused their requests.

After her tour of the Californian mining camps, Lola returned to San Francisco. Managers and audiences were pleased to see her again, and when her popularity eventually started to wane, she decided to continue her world tour by crossing the Pacific Ocean to Australia.

CHAPTER TWENTY-SIX

Lance Devlin

LOLA set about organising the visit to Australia, and she appointed an ex-army officer, Lance Devlin, to act as her agent.

She first made Devlin's acquaintance one evening in the dining room of the Golden Gate Hotel. She was dining alone when a tall, well-built man approached her table.

"Excuse me, ma'am, but all the other tables are taken. May I share yours?"

Lola looked up at the stranger. He had a friendly smile, and she felt instantly attracted to him. "Sure," she replied. "Please take a seat. I always welcome company."

"Thank you, ma'am," said the gentleman, seating himself opposite her at the table. "Allow me to introduce myself. My name is Lance Devlin."

"Pleased to meet you, Lance. My name is Lola."

"Yes, I know who you are. You're Lola Montez, Countess of Landsfeld. I saw you perform on stage last night."

"I hope you enjoyed my performance. Tell me, Lance, what is your profession?"

Devlin laughed. "I was formerly a Captain in the United States Army. Unfortunately my superior officer discovered that I was having an affair with his wife, and he challenged me to a duel. I shot him, and was court-martialed."

"What have you been doing since you left the Army, Lance?"

Devlin flashed his white teeth in a grin. "I must confess that I am currently unemployed."

"Perhaps I could offer you a job."

"What sort of job?"

"I am currently trying to organise a theatrical troupe to visit Australia, and I require an agent to arrange things. You seem to be a capable gentleman. Would you be interested in accepting a position as my agent?"

"Yes, I would."

"Good," said Lola. "We can discuss the details tomorrow."

Lola enjoyed a pleasant meal with Lance Devlin, and after they had finished dessert, she said, "I have enjoyed your company, Lance. Would you like to come up to my room for a nightcap?"

"Sure," replied Lance, who was under no illusion as to why she had invited him. This was not the first time that a lady had been charmed by his rugged good looks.

Devlin accompanied Lola up to her hotel suite. The rooms were large and lavishly furnished.

"Would you like a glass of champagne?" she asked.

"I wouldn't mind," he replied.

Lola popped the cork of a bottle of champagne, pouring the bubbling liquid into two thin-stemmed glasses, handing one to Lance and taking the other for herself.

"Here's to us, Lance," she said, clinking her glass against his.

"To us, Lola," he replied.

After they had drunk the champagne, Lola threw an enquiring glance at Lance. He smiled back, and without more ado, she slid into his arms, molding her slim body against his.

"Kiss me, Lance," she whispered.

He covered her lips with his, kissing her long and passionately.

Lola could feel his fierce erection pressing against her belly through their clothing, and she suddenly dropped to her knees in front of him, her deft fingers eagerly unfastening the buttons of his fly. Her hand reached inside his trousers, pulling out his swollen pego.

"Oh, what have we here?" she exclaimed, popping her lips over his empurpled glans.

She took Lance's shaft deep into the moist cavity of her mouth, moving her head back and forth, her tongue swirling against the sensitive underside of his turgid knob.

Devlin gasped in breathless delight as Lola's liquid lips and talented tongue pleasured his upstanding member. The sensation was so voluptuous that he was tempted to spurt off inside her mouth, but he somehow managed to control himself, pushing her head away from his twitching cock at the last moment.

"Let's get our clothes off," said Lola, starting to unfastened the buttons down the front of her dress.

When they were both naked, Devlin lifted Lola in his arms, carrying her into the adjoining bedroom. He threw her down onto the large bed, and then climbed on top of her shapely body.

Positioning the knob of his shaft between the moist, slippery folds of her juicy quim, he penetrated her with one smooth thrust.

"Oh, yes, yes!" sighed Lola as Devlin started to ram his cock in and out of her clasping sheath, his balls smacking against the plump cheeks of her bottom.

She ran her hands up and down the length of his back as he worked away on top of her, her fingers fluttering like butterflies from his broad shoulders down to his taut buttocks. She undulated her hips, moaning with pleasure as Devlin speeded up the pace of his strokes.

"Oh—oh—ooohhh!" gasped Lola. "I'm about to come!! OH, YES, YES!!!"

She wrapped her long legs about his waist, locking her ankles together against the small of his back, as her body went into convulsions, wracked by one delicious spasm after another.

A second later, Devlin joined her in blissful release, his spunk spurting out, flooding the inmost recesses of her cunt.

After this delightful bout of pleasure, they lay together in each other's arms for some while until they had both recovered from their exertions and were ready for another amorous combat.

Their second course was even more enjoyable than the first. This time they were able to hold back their climaxes much longer before being overwhelmed by the blissful convulsions of the supreme moment.

In the sweet aftermath of their pleasure, as they lay together in one another's arms, Lola said, "Lance, you are a wonderful lover, and no mistake."

They had already enjoyed two bouts of pleasure, but the night was still young. Before long the two of them were writhing together in the delightful transports of yet another glorious fuck.

CHAPTER TWENTY-SEVEN

Down Under

LOLA MONTEZ and Lance Devlin left San Francisco early in June on the *Southern Star*, and on arrival in Sydney, they recruited a small company of local actors. The first play performed by the company was *Lola Montez in Bavaria* at the Royal Victoria Theatre in Sydney, which attracted large audiences.

After Sydney, they travelled down to Melbourne in the Port Phillip district where *Lola Montez in Bavaria* was again performed, this time at the Theatre Royal. When the audiences started to decline after a month, Lola placed an advertisement in the daily newspapers announcing that, in between acts, she would perform "The Celebrated Spider Dance".

That night the theatre was stacked to full capacity, and even though the dance performed by Lola was not so salacious as the one performed in the Californian goldfields, it was still risqué enough to be condemned by Dr. John Lawrence Milton, head of the City Court Mission.

Dr. Milton, who prided himself on being a champion of morals, appeared at the Melbourne Police Court and applied for a warrant for the arrest of Lola Montez, on the grounds that her Spider Dance had "outraged decency".

The Mayor of Melbourne, John Thomas Smith, was the presiding magistrate, however, and he disliked sanctimonious preachers who told other people how they should behave.

"Did you actually witness the performance?" the Mayor asked.

"No, I did not," replied Dr. Milton, offended by the question. "I am not in the habit of watching obscene dances."

"Can you produce any witnesses who were offended by the Spider Dance?"

"I am sure I can find some, Your Honour."

"You mean you don't have any witnesses at the present time. In that case, there is no way I can issue a warrant for Madame Montez's arrest. Please do not come back here until you have found some witnesses to corroborate your unsubstantiated accusation."

Dr. Milton was not happy with this response, and he went away in a bad temper, determined to find some witnesses to support his complaint.

However, before he could produce any witnesses, Lola instructed her lawyers to serve a writ for criminal libel upon the reverend minister.

As a result, Dr. Milton, who did not wish to become involved in a lawsuit which might end badly for him, chose not to pursue the matter any further.

Lola was understandably grateful to the Mayor for having refused to issue a warrant for her arrest. She wrote a letter to him expressing her gratitude, and inviting him to have supper with her. He replied that he would be happy to accept her invitation.

They dined together after her next stage performance, and before the night was over, she had added another conquest to her long list of lovers.

CHAPTER TWENTY-EIGHT

Countess de Chabrillan

LOLA MONTEZ was strolling down Swanston Street, the main street of Melbourne, one afternoon when she was totally surprised to see Celeste Mogador coming towards her.

"Celeste, what are you doing here in Melbourne?" Lola asked.

"I could ask you the same thing," replied Celeste. "I know that you were offered an engagement in New York, but Melbourne is a long way from New York."

"Let's go into a coffee shop," said Lola, "and we can exchange stories."

When they were seated at a table and had ordered two cups of coffee and some biscuits, Lola told her friend that, after her successful tours of the major cities of the United States, she had decided to go to Australia, where she had been equally successful in drawing large audiences.

At the conclusion of Lola's account of her adventures, Celeste said, "Well, I guess it's my turn now to explain why I am here in Melbourne."

"Yes, I'm all ears. Please tell me."

"Well, after you departed from Paris for New York, I met a young man, Lionel de Chabrillan, and we fell in love. He didn't mind that I was a prostitute, and he asked me to marry him. His family was a very aristocratic one, however, and were opposed to the marriage. In order to prevent the marriage from going ahead, his family arranged for him to be appointed to the post of French Consul in Melbourne.

"His family thought that they could keep Lionel out of my clutches by sending him to Australia on the other side of the world, but they were wrong. Lionel married me before leaving France for Australia, and took me with him.

"I should add that, shortly after our arrival in Melbourne, Lionel received news that his father, the Count de Chabrillan, had died, and that Lionel had inherited the title and attached estates."

"Do you mean to say that you are now a countess?"

"Yes, I'm a countess, just like you."

"You have certainly moved up in the world, Celeste."

"Yes, I have achieved my ambition to marry into wealth and luxury. I should add, however, that I am in no way ashamed of the fact that I once worked as a prostitute. In fact, I have already started to write my memoirs, describing my past career as a lady of pleasure."

After they had talked for a while, Lola invited Celeste and her husband to have supper with her after her performance that evening at the Theatre Royal.

They had supper in the private room of a nearby restaurant, and after a few glasses of wine, Lionel said to Lola, "Celeste tells me that you worked in the same profession as her in Paris."

"Yes, that's right. I didn't have any theatrical engagements, and I had to work as a high class prostitute in order to support myself. In fact, Celeste and I shared a client one night. We had the same pimp and he found a client for us who wanted to have sex with two girls at the one time. The client was an Englishman who was willing to pay generously, and I must say the three of us had a most enjoyable night together."

Lionel had listened with interest to Lola's story.

"It seems like you had a lot of fun," he remarked. "That gives me an idea. Lola, why don't you, me and Celeste have a threesome like the one you have just described. What do you say?"

"I think that's a capital idea," Lola replied. "We could all go to my hotel. The bed in my room is big enough for the three of us."

Celeste seconded her husband's suggestion, and they left the restaurant, hailing a cab which took them to Lola's hotel.

There they spent the night in a wild orgy of licentious pleasure, and did not wake up next morning until midday.

122

CHAPTER TWENTY-NINE

Captain Starlight

FROM MELBOURNE Lola Montez proceeded to the Ballarat goldfields. The miners came from all over the world, and included criminals and escaped convicts, but she moved among them freely and unafraid.

She performed at the Victoria Theatre in Ballarat, and was applauded loudly by the audience. Little known by either Lola or anyone else, one of the audience was the notorious bushranger, Captain Starlight, whose gang had been active in the Port Phillip district for the past three years.

The gang had held up stagecoaches, robbed banks and raided the homesteads of wealthy pastoralists. So far, all the efforts of local police officers to capture the gang had failed.

After the performance, Captain Starlight returned to his gang's hideout, which was located in the hills to the north of Ballarat.

"Boys, I've thought of another way to get our hands on some money," he told the gang members.

"What's that?" asked Dingo Bill.

"We're going to kidnap Lola Montez, the famous actress, who is currently performing at the Victoria Theatre in Ballarat, and hold her for ransom. I read about her in the newspapers, and last night I attended a play starring her. She is incredibly popular. There was not a vacant seat in the theatre, and if we were to abduct her, I reckon we could demand £1,000 for her release."

"But who's going to pay the ransom?"

"I'm sure the theatre manager will agree to pay it. At last night's performance, there were over two thousand spectators in the theatre, mostly miners, and they all cheered and applauded her. Lola draws large audiences, and over the past month, she must have received several thousand pounds as her share of the ticket sales. The theatre manager's share would have been much larger. He should be able to pay the ransom without any trouble."

"How exactly do you plan to kidnap her?" asked another member of the gang. "We can't just snatch her off the stage of the Victoria Theatre."

"No, we can't. We'll just bide our time," replied Captain Starlight. "We'll keep an eye on her, and sooner or later an opportunity will present itself. Once we've got her, we'll bring her back here to the hideout, and hold her until the ransom is paid."

CHAPTER THIRTY

Kidnapped!

THE TOWN of Ballarat is located around the shore of Lake Wendouree, and in the afternoons, Lola sometimes went for walks around the lake.

The lake was a large one and the walk around it took about an hour. One afternoon, she had reached the far side of the lake when a coach suddenly drew up beside her, and two men jumped out.

They ran towards her, and before she had time to flee, they seized her and dragged her towards the coach.

"Let me go!" she screamed, struggling to free herself from their clutches. "Get your hands off me!"

"Gag her!" ordered one of the men, and his companion stuffed a handkerchief into her mouth to stifle her screams.

When they reached the coach, the two men forced her inside. They seated themselves on either side of her, holding her firmly so that she could not escape.

A third man was on the box of the coach. He whipped the horses and the coach was soon speeding along the road that led north from Ballarat.

The land to either side of the road was flat, but after three hours the coach reached some forested hills. After another half-hour, the coach stopped in front of a shack, and the men told Lola to get out.

Captain Starlight emerged from the shack, and came towards the coach.

"So you were able to snatch her," he said. "Good work, boys."

After she got out of the coach, Lola collapsed on the ground, staring up at the looming figure of Captain Starlight, who was standing over her, his feet set well apart.

"Why have you kidnapped me?" she asked. "What do you want with me?"

"The answer to that is simple, Lola. I'm going to demand a ransom for your release. Unless the ransom is paid, you'll never see your friends again."

"You'll won't get away with this, you villain!"

Starlight laughed aloud. "I beg to differ, Madame. I'm sure the manager of the Victoria Theatre will agree to anything to get you back. But in the meantime, I think I might have myself some fun."

Lola was still sprawled on the ground, staring up at the bushranger. In her struggles, her dress had become torn and was hanging in tatters from her shoulders. One breast was fully exposed.

Captain Starlight could not take his gaze off the luscious spectacle. He licked his lips, his eyes blazing with animal passion.

Lola cowered back from his brutish glare, recognizing the lustful intent in his eyes.

"Don't you dare touch me!" she cried.

"Real little spitfire, ain't you?" drawled Starlight. "All right, boys, hold her down! I'm going to fuck the bitch!"

126

Each of the gang seized one of Lola's limbs, holding her spreadeagled body down on the ground. The bushranger then leant over her, ripping the clothes from her struggling body. The alabaster flesh of her naked body gleamed in the bright sunlight.

Lola's eyes fastened on Starlight, and she watched in fear as he unbuttoned the fly of his trousers, pulling out his cock, which was already fully erect. Kneeling between Lola's splayed thighs, he rubbed the head of his prick back and forth between the slippery lips of her vulva.

The actress tried to struggle when she realized that he was about to penetrate her, but Starlight struck her in the face with his clenched fist.

Lola's senses reeled from the blow, and in another moment her attacker had lunged forward with his hips, driving his cock home to the hilt.

"Honey, there is only one thing I enjoy more than fucking a willing lady, and that's fucking an *unwilling* one!" said the bushranger with a big grin.

Starlight proceeded to ram his cock in and out of Lola's cunt with fierce, shuddering strokes, and it did not take him long to finish the job, spurting off after only one or two minutes.

"Can the rest of us have a turn now, boss?" asked Dingo Bill.

"Sure," replied Starlight, climbing to his feet and pushing his cock back inside his trousers. "Do what you like with her!"

"Thanks, boss!" cried Dingo Bill, eagerly stripping off his trousers and throwing himself on top of the actress.

127

After he had finished with Lola, the other members of the gang took their pleasure of their captive. Lola endured her ordeal bravely, and when the last of her attackers had spurted off inside her belly, she thought that her ordeal must now surely be over. But she was badly mistaken.

"Get down on your hands and knees now, madame!" said Starlight, unbuttoning the fly of his trousers for the second time.

Lola did as she was told, and Starlight knelt behind her, spitting on her anus to lubricate it. He then pressed the engorged head of his iron-hard shaft against the puckered orifice.

"No, no, don't!" screamed Lola, looking back anxiously over her shoulder. She had been fucked in the bottom only once before in her life, and she had not enjoyed the experience. "You mustn't! Please don't!"

"Shut up, you bitch!" snarled Starlight as he forced his cock slowly into Lola's asshole.

As her anal sheath was tight and dry, the relentless advance of Starlight's shaft into her rectum caused Lola to sob in pain. She begged the bushranger to stop, but he ignored her cries for mercy.

Gripping her hips firmly between his strong hands, Starlight uttered a cruel laugh as he proceeded to bugger Lola with long, deep strokes.

Meanwhile, Dingo Bill had moved around in front of the kneeling female. He forced his cock into her mouth, telling her to suck him off.

Lola no longer tried to resist. She realized that all struggle was useless, and she thought that her best course of action was to obey any command given her, so as to end her suffering as quickly as possible.

Starlight and Dingo Bill fucked her in the ass and the mouth with savage glee, spurting off within a few seconds of each other. Starlight flooded Lola's asshole with jet after jet of warm, sticky spunk, and at almost the same instant, Bill came in her mouth, forcing her to swallow every drop of his sizzling spunk.

After Starlight and his lieutenant had slaked their vicious desires, Lola could scarcely move. Her naked body was torn and bleeding, and she was barely conscious of her surroundings.

Some minutes passed before she recovered her senses sufficiently to climb unsteadily to her feet. She found her clothes and struggled back into them, glaring at her captors with hate-filled eyes.

"What are you going to do with me now?" she demanded.

"Lock you up in the shack," replied Starlight. "You'll stay there until the ransom is paid. Like I said before, I'm sure the manager of the Victoria Theatre will be willing to pay to get you back."

"Maybe he will, maybe he won't," said Lola. "I don't trust him. Send the ransom note to my agent, Lance Devlin. Once he knows I've been kidnapped, he'll definitely agree to pay the ransom."

After they had locked her up, Captain Starlight sat down at a desk and wrote the ransom note. He reread the note several times before folding it and sealing it in an envelope.

The next morning he gave the note to Dingo Bill and One-Eyed Mick, telling them to ride to Ballarat and give it to Lance Devlin.

CHAPTER THIRTY-ONE

The Shoot Out

DINGO BILL and One-Eyed Mick delivered the ransom note at noon, and rode off before Devlin could open it. When he took the note out of the sealed envelope, he read the following:

"DEVLIN——My gang are holding Lola Montez prisoner. If you want to get her back alive, you'll have to pay £1,000. Two of my boys will be waiting at the ten mile post on the road north of Ballarat at eight o'clock this evening. Come alone to give them the money and I will release her tomorrow morning. Do not tell the police if you want to ever see her again. "CAPTAIN STARLIGHT"

Devlin already knew that Lola had been missing since the previous afternoon, and he had spent the night and morning searching for her, but without success. He now knew that she had been abducted by Captain Starlight, and he wracked his brain, thinking of what he should do.

He thought that, even if he handed over £1,000 to the bushrangers, there was no guarantee that the gang would release Lola. In fact, she might already be dead.

After some consideration, Devlin decided upon a course of action.

He hired a horse from the local livery stable, and reached the ten mile post at the appointed time. A bright moon was overhead and he could see two men standing beside the road. Two horses were tethered nearby.

Devlin rode slowly towards the men.

"Have you brought the money?" called out Dingo Bill.

"Yes, I've got it in my coat pocket."

"Well, hand it over."

"Sure," replied Devlin, his hand reaching inside his pocket.

A moment later, he whipped out a Colt revolver and squeezed the trigger. The first bullet struck Dingo Bill in the forehead, killing him instantly. The second bullet hit One-Eyed Mick in the shoulder, causing him to drop his pistol.

Devlin had deliberately refrained from killing the second bushranger, because he wanted to question him. The wounded man was sprawled out on the ground, moaning in pain.

"I've got a question to ask you," said Devlin, placing the muzzle of his revolver against the side of the bushranger's skull. "If you don't answer it, I'll put a bullet in your head. Where is Lola Montez? You've got exactly ten seconds to talk and then I'll pull this trigger. One, two, three—"

One-Eyed Mick swallowed hard. "I'm not telling you anything, Devlin."

"—four, five, six—"

Lance Devlin's voice was cold and devoid of emotion as he counted out the seconds.

"Go to hell! I'm not saying a word!"

"—seven, eight, nine—"

"All right, all right, don't shoot! I'll tell you where she is. There's an old shack up in the hills. That's our hideout. Captain Starlight is holding her there."

"How do I find the shack?" demanded Lance. "Tell me quick!"

The wounded bushranger turned towards the hills, pointing at two peaks which were faintly outlined against the moonlit sky.

"See those two peaks. Ride straight towards them. You'll find the shack in a gully between them."

"You'd better not be lying. If you are, I'll come back and put another bullet in you!"

"I'm not lying."

Devlin tied One-Eyed Mck to the trunk of a gumtree, and then mounted his horse. He raked the sides of the horse with his spurs, riding towards the hills at a gallop.

Two hour's hard riding brought him to the gully, and he rode slowly along it, looking for the shack. He had to rein his horse to a halt several times because the moon had gone behind a cloud, forcing him to wait until the moon reappeared, illuminating the valley in a ghostly light.

It took an hour for Devlin to find the wooden shack. The shack was located beside a narrow creek, which gleamed in the moonlight like a ribbon of quicksilver.

Swinging out of his saddle, Devlin tethered his horse to a tree and ran forward on foot. He moved swiftly and silently towards the shack.

Yellow light spilled from the windows, and it was obvious that the shack was occupied. He peered in through one of the windows, keeping his head above the sill only long enough for a quick look inside.

One look was enough. Lola was tied securely to a chair in the middle of the shack. She seemed to have dozed off, and only her bonds kept her upright.

Captain Starlight and two men were seated around a table, playing a game of cards. They were smoking cigars, and a half-empty bottle of whisky was on the table.

"Bill and Mick should be back soon with the ransom money," remarked one of the men.

"Yeah, in a couple of hours," said Captain Starlight.

"What are we going to do with the famous Lola Montez once we have the money?"

"We could escort her back to Ballarat and release her on the outskirts of the town, but why should we go to all that trouble," said Starlight. "We'll fuck her another couple of times, then just shoot her, and bury her body someplace where it will never be found!"

At that instant, Lance Devlin kicked open the door, bursting into the shack. He was holding a Colt revolver in each hand, and he levelled them at the three bushrangers.

"This is the end of your career as a bushranger, Captain Starlight," said Devlin. "You and your boys, line up against that wall with your hands up above your heads. Now!"

The three outlaws did as they were ordered, while Devlin kept them covered with one revolver. He

134

slipped his other revolver back into its holster, and pulled out a Bowie knife with his free hand. He slashed Lola's bonds with two cuts of the razor-sharp blade.

Lance stepped back from the chair as Lola stumbled to her feet, trying to rub the circulation back into her numb hands.

"Oh, thank heavens!" she cried. "You've rescued me, Lance. How can I ever thank you?"

She crossed the room towards her rescuer, who still had the three bushrangers covered with his revolver. Unfortunately, in moving forward, Lola unwittingly obstructed Lance's line of fire.

"Get him, boys," shouted Captain Starlight, taking advantage of this unexpected opportunity. His two men instantly obeyed, reaching for the revolvers in the holsters on their hips.

But they were not quite quick enough. They had barely cleared leather when Devlin shot first one and then the other. Blood spurted from the bullet holes, and they were dead before their bodies hit the floor.

In the confusion, however, Captain Starlight had been able to seize Lola, and he now held her in front of himself with one arm, while pressing the muzzle of a pistol against her temple with his free hand.

"Drop your revolver, or I'll kill her!" ordered Starlight.

Lola's eyes were looking directly at Devlin, pleading with him to do as the bushranger demanded.

"Do it!" screamed Starlight. "Or I'll shoot the bitch right now!"

Lance Devlin opened his fingers slowly, letting the revolver fall from his hand. After the pistol hit the floor, Starlight pushed Lola away from himself. She collided with the wall and slid down it.

She was sprawled out full length on the floor, but raised herself on her hands, staring with wild-eyed horror at the scene around her. She could see Devlin's revolver lying on the floor only a few yards away, and she dazedly crawled towards it.

Captain Starlight was grinning in triumph. He extended his arm, aiming his pistol carefully at Lance Devlin.

"You're a dead man!" he said, his finger tightening on the trigger.

Devlin waited without flinching for the bullet to hit him.

A shot rang out, deafeningly loud in the confined space of the shack. But the shot did not come from Starlight's revolver.

Lance Devlin stared in astonishment as Captain Starlight's lifeless body crashed to the floor and lay still. Lance's eyes then found Lola, who was on her knees, clasping Devlin's revolver in both hands. She fired a second bullet into the bushranger's body, then a third. She kept squeezing the trigger even when the revolver was empty, the gun hammer clicking harmlessly on spent cartridges.

Devlin took the revolver from her hands, and helped her to her feet.

"Are you all right, Lola," he asked her.

"Yes, I'm all right," she replied. "I'm happy to say that the same can't be said for Captain Starlight! I enjoyed killing the bastard!"

CHAPTER THIRTY-TWO

Last Days

AFTER leaving Australia, Lola Montez and Lance Devlin travelled to Shanghai, Calcutta, Bombay and Cairo before arriving back in the United States.

Lola was now forty years old, and her body was not as supple as it had once been. She could no longer perform dances with the same virtuosity as in her younger years, and she realized that she would have to find some other source of income.

By good fortune, she met an evangelistic clergyman, the Rev. Charles Chauncy Burr, who suggested that they should go on a lecture tour together. Her new career began in May 1857 at the Broadway Theatre in New York, and was quite successful.

Charles Burr wrote the lectures and Lola delivered them. The lectures had such titles as "Beautiful Women", "Gallantry", "Heroines of History", "Comic Aspects of Love" and "Wits and Women of Paris". The lectures attracted good audiences, because of Lola's notoriety, and were published as a book in 1858 by the New York publisher, Rudd and Carleton.

After their success in New York, the couple embarked on a lecture tour of the British Isles in 1858, and did not return to New York until November 1859.

Unfortunately, the next fourteen months were tragic ones for Lola Montez. She contracted a serious illness, and did not recover. She died on the 17th January 1861 in a cheap tenement room in the New York slum area known as Hell's Kitchen. She was buried in Greenwood Cemetery in Brooklyn.

Lola Montez was only forty-two years old when she died, but by then her fame had spread throughout the countries of the Western world. She had been a welcome guest in the royal courts of Europe, and her many lovers had included Czar Nicholas I of Russia, King Ludwig I of Bavaria, and such celebrities as the famous French author, Alexandre Dumas.

No other courtesan has ever attracted so much public attention as Lola Montez, and many books have been written about her. She was a courageous champion of democratic government and liberty, but she is chiefly remembered today as one of the most notorious courtesans of the 19th century!

THE END

ACKNOWLEDGEMENTS

In writing *The Notorious Lola Montez*, the author has relied upon a number of sources for details of Lola's early life and later career. He would like to acknowledge his indebtedness to the following works in particular:

Lola Montez, *The Lectures of Lola Montez (Countess of Landsfeld) including her Autobiography*, Rudd & Carleton, New York, 1858.

Edmund B. D'Auvergne, *Lola Montez, An Adventuress of the Forties*, T. Werner Laurie Ltd, London 1909.

T. Everett Harré, *The Heavenly Sinner, The Life and Loves of Lola Montez*, The Macaulay Company, New York, 1935.

Horace Wyndham, *The Magnificent Montez, From Courtesan to Convert*, Hutchinson & Co, London, 1935.

Anonymous, *Lola Montes, The Tragic Story of a 'Liberated Woman'*, Heritage Publications, Melbourne, 1973.

ABOUT THE AUTHOR

JACK FALWORTH is a writer of erotic novels and other pulp fiction. He especially admires the classic novels of Victorian erotica, which have had a strong influence on his own literary works.

Jack strives to write fast moving stories with strong plot lines and a wide variety of sexual situations. His aim is to entertain, and he would welcome any comments his readers might care to offer on the products of his vivid imagination.

———————

Readers are welcome to contact Jack directly at the following email address:

jackfalworth@outlook.com

Readers who would like to write a review of any of his novels may do so on the website where the novel was purchased.

OTHER PAPERBACKS BY JACK FALWORTH

BLUE BLOOD NYMPHO

Set in the 1890s, this novel describes the sexual adventures of Miss Lorelei Langley, a member of the London fast set. Lorelei is bored with life in London's social circles, and she decides to visit the Australian colonies. Lorelei has a constant itch between her legs, and while she is in Australia, she never misses an opportunity to hop into bed with any handsome man who takes her fancy. Her many lovers include His Excellency Lord Amberly, Governor of the Colony of Victoria.

NYMPHO NIGHTS

This is the second novel of a series describing the sexual adventures of Miss Lorelei Langley in 19th century Australia. After her erotic escapades in Melbourne, Lorelei travels to Sydney, where she adds more lovers to her list of conquests.

PLEASURES OF A LIBERTINE

Set in Victorian England, this novel describes the amorous adventures of Frank Mortimer, a wealthy young libertine. Many of his sexual encounters involve prostitutes, but he also charms his way into the beds of a remarkable number of maidservants, titled ladies and even an Italian Countess.

FROM VIRGIN TO PORN STAR

Holly Carson is an eighteen year old girl from a town in the American mid-West who is eager to lose her virginity. After seducing her stepfather, she is thrown out of home by her mother. Holly then heads for Los Angeles where she finds work—first as a stripper and later as a porn actress. She is a big hit in X-rated movies, and within twelve months she is one of America's top porn stars!

CAMPUS CHICK

Astri is an Indonesian college student who works part-time as a high class callgirl in order to pay her tuition fees. Her clients include a wide range of wealthy and important men who pay her generously for her services. Astri enjoys her work as a callgirl, but her college marks suffer as a result. However, she still graduates with top honors from her course— after bribing the College Dean with her sexual favors!

WANTON QUEEN OF ZORAKH

Kitty Adair, star reporter of the *London Daily Bugle*, accompanies the famous African hunter and explorer, Allan Quatermain, on an expedition to find the fabled lost city of Zorakh. The pulp fiction plot of this spicy adventure story is interlaced with lots of gratuitous sex. The sexual exploits of the wanton Queen of Zorakh, the oversexed Kitty and the lecherous Quatermain are all described in explicit detail.

LECHEROUS LIAISONS

A long and carefully researched erotic novel by Jack Falworth, describing the sexual adventures of Harry Hotspur, a young Victorian rogue. Harry is ruthless in his pursuit of licentious pleasure, and his many conquests include various maidservants, a country wench, a vicar's daughter, numerous prostitutes, a famous stage actress and a German princess.

TROPIC POLICE GIRL

This novel is an erotic murder mystery featuring Sergeant Ayesha Asmara, a young and very sexy Indonesian policewoman. Ayesha is involved in investigating the murder of a university lecturer, and she soon discovers that the lecturer was running an online prostitution service. One of the murder suspects is the owner of an illegal massage parlor, and Ayesha goes undercover, working as a massage parlor girl in order to gather evidence. Ayesha solves the murder, but not before she has enjoyed a number of steamy sexual encounters with members of both sexes.

HOT NIGHTS IN BALI

Another novel in the erotic murder mystery series featuring Indonesian policewoman Sergeant Ayesha Asmara. In the latest story, Ayesha investigates the murder of a best-selling American novelist on the island of Bali. The novelist was not well liked, and there are numerous suspects, including his sexy wife, a lecherous Australian senator and a gay freelance journalist.

MATA HARI EXOTIC TEMPTRESS

Mata Hari was an erotic dancer and high class prostitute who was wrongly accused of being a German spy and executed by firing squad during the First World War. This carefully researched novel by Jack Falworth is a sexually explicit account of her spectacular career, her many love affairs, and the events leading up to her betrayal by the French Secret Service.

PERILS OF A COURTESAN

The Countess du Barry was the Royal Mistress of Louis XV of France. Jack Falworth's explicit account of her life describes her humble origins, her career as a high-class prostitute, her activities at the French Court, and finally, the last years of her life before she was dragged, screaming, to the guillotine.

WHITE SLAVES OF ALGIERS

Set in the late 19th century, this X-rated novel tells the story of Rosa Spedwick, an English girl, who is abducted by a white slave syndicate and forced to become a prostitute in an Algiers brothel. She is rescued by an English sailor, and returns to England, where she smashes the syndicate.

UNLEASHED PASSION

A collection of ten erotic short stories by Jack Falworth. Most of the stories have contemporary settings while others are set in Victorian England. They contain explicit accounts of masturbation, defloration, straight sex, oral sex, sodomy, seduction, lesbianism and prostitution.

Printed in Great Britain
by Amazon

18338431R00088